SLITHER

VALARIE SAVAGE KINNEY

Twisted Core Press, LLC.

ISBN-13: 978-0692483572 (Twisted Core Press)

ISBN-10: 0692483578

SLITHER

©2015 Valarie Savage Kinney All rights reserved. No part of this book may be reproduced or transferred without the express written consent of the author.

Published by

Twisted Core Press, LLC.

Smithfield, NC

This is a work of fiction. Any similarity with real persons or events is purely coincidental. Persons, events, and locations are either the product of the author's imagination, or used fictitiously.

Image Artist: Gromovataya

Cover Design: Twisted Core Press, LLC

Edited by: Jennifer Welborn

SLITHER

Dedication

For my husband, John

Always. Forever.

And always again.

For my children

Olivia, Savannah, Donovan, and Brennan

Every moment I've spent with you

Has been worth a thousand days spent in the presence

Of anyone else.

For Carsen Shane, Emmett Dale, Kayla Christine, and Avira Irene

You are the sunshine of our tomorrows

And our tomorrows have never looked brighter.

And for Hunter Glen

Who is my hero.

Valerie Savage Kinney

Chapter One

There's No Place Like Home.

"*Sing me a song
Of a lass that is gone
Say, could that lass
Be I?*"
–Bear McCreary, *Skye Boat Song*

Zari clawed at her sister, Gianna, in a desperate attempt to escape. Gianna ran her forked tongue slowly across her upper lip. The slimy, berry-colored muscle dripped hot saliva onto Zari's face as she turned away from Gianna's menacing glare. "Please don't make me watch! I don't want to see this again!" Zari cried, curling into a ball on the hard, cold floor of the shed.

Nan stomped on Zari's stomach, anger flushing her grizzled features. "Listen, you little bitch. You will sit still and watch, or I will see to it your father beats you senseless...again. Remember the last time?" Zari did remember. She'd not been able to walk for two days after the last beating. The pain in her gut now was so great it knocked the air from her lungs as she wheezed.

Zari whimpered. Pain, shame and disgust clenched her stomach as the young man tied to the pallet in the corner screamed for mercy. Pop straddled the man, laughing as his prisoner frantically thrashed about. Nan and Gianna gripped Zari's arms and forced her to a sitting position. Roughly grabbing her chin,

Nan yanked her head forward. "Watch!" Nan hissed.

Terror shook Zari's bones, leaving her shivering as she raised her eyes to the scene in the corner of the shed. Pop ran his thumb over the lips of the man, who cried out once more but was quickly silenced when the snake burst forth from Pop's mouth and slithered down the throat of the man, a drifter who had stopped by the farmhouse the day before, looking for work.

The man's body had stilled and dark, thick rivers of blood dripped from his mouth and nose down the side of his face. Pop's mouth pressed against the lips of the stranger as the serpent fed. When her father finally rose, the snake slid back into his mouth and Pop wiped the blood from his lips with the back of his hand. He met Zari's gray-green eyes with his own, and grinned. His teeth were stained dark red.

Gianna's split tongue flicked against Zari's ear; the feel of the wet, dual points of it against her skin made Zari flinch. "Soon," Gianna whispered, tracing the outer edge of Zari's ear with her tongue. "Soon, it will be your turn to feed."

Pop shoved the limp body of the young man onto the pile of human shells stacked along the wall of the shed.

Overwhelmed by the stench of blood and decaying flesh, Zari began to vomit. Vile chunks of rancid meat erupted from her mouth and bile burned her throat and nose as she heaved. Grimacing, she dragged the hem of her shirt across her mouth, resolving never to eat meat again.

~***~

"You cannot escape who you are!"

Pop's parting words echoed in her mind as Zari adjusted her oversized bag – the multi-colored one with the peace sign on it – and slapped her purple flip-flops against the hard-packed earth. The wind picked up and her peasant skirt twirled in the breeze.

Almost home.

So many memories. So many years, lost. It had shredded her heart to leave her family home, but it had been the only way. Zari shook her head, clearing the cobwebs of the past and focusing instead on the present. She rubbed the underside of the silver ring on the third finger of her left hand. She smiled as she turned in to her driveway.

Home.

Home.

~***~

Stepping into the house, Zari peeked around the kitchen wall and saw Emmett asleep in his dark brown recliner. Newspaper across his lap, glasses resting low on his nose, shaggy brown hair curling up in random wisps. Tenderly, she smiled. Together nearly four years now, she was still sometimes struck by her luck in finding him. She loved him so much, and she loved him enough to feel guilt thick and heavy in her gut when she allowed herself to think of what she was keeping from him. *I don't need to tell him because I left it all behind. I can control it. It's not a lie.*

Emmett stirred and rubbed his eyes, blinking at the sun streaming through the windows. He caught sight of her and grinned, his one very crooked eyetooth adding to his somewhat rakish appearance. With a few long strides, Zari perched on the arm of his chair, her hand resting easily on the back of his head.

"How was it? Sell much?"

"Market was busy today. I sold a few quilts, a couple of baby blankets. It was a good day."

"I'm so proud of you, babe. Your work is amazing, and I can't believe what you can make with your hands. So much talent." He held her hands in his and squeezed.

Zari laughed. "That's debatable. All right, I'm going to get dinner started. Let me up."

Singing bits and pieces of favorite songs as she worked, Zari swayed to her own music as she chopped vegetables for salad and stirred pasta in the pot bubbling with water.

Her hand was shaking again, a steady tremor from fingertip to elbow. Taking a deep breath, she held the rest of her body perfectly still in an effort to stop the twitching. She set the knife on the counter. This was happening too often, and Zari didn't know why. She should tell Emmett, but she didn't want to worry him and she surely wasn't planning to go to the doctor. No telling what they might find.

The sun was low in the wide expanse of purple, pink and orange, and Zari stood on their generous back porch taking in the colors of the night sky. With the moments until darkness running short, a chill rushed through the air that was laced with the scent of lilacs and she pulled her shawl closer around her shivering body. Light footsteps fell on the wooden boards behind her, *one, two, three,* and Emmett was warm against her back, his long, muscled arms encircling her, pulling her back toward him. He buried his face in her neck, dropping light kisses from ear to shoulder. Zari murmured with pleasure and turned to him, meeting his mouth with hers, wet and hot. Working quickly, she unbuttoned his shirt with an efficiency that spoke of experience and a quick thrill shot through her body, as it always did, at the sight of the dark green, barbed wire tattoos that laced his upper arms. Exploring his bare skin was pure lightning, jolts and heat and storms that sent thoughts scattering and left only desire as they tumbled onto the wooden deck, need meeting need. Emmett reached up and ripped the scarf from her head, rejoicing in the explosion of dirty blond dreads that fell past her hips when she was upright, but seemed to be everywhere now, as their bodies twisted in passion on the deck of the old farmhouse.

Zari's shawl danced in the wind as it slid around the railing and down the steps, caught up in its own music.

~***~

"Pack me a lunch?" His voice was filled with sleep yet, his shirt still unbuttoned. With a drowsy smile, Emmett reached for Zari and she slipped her fingers into his with a tight squeeze then released to button his shirt for him, a penance to the universe for their union last night under the stars where anyone, *anything*, could have seen them.

"Of course. What kind of wife do you think I am?" Her voice was deep, a hoarse, throaty sound that sent a spark through Emmett every time she spoke.

"Got your laptop?"

"Yes."

"Graded homework?"

"I do."

"Wallet? Cellphone?"

Emmett patted the pockets of his not entirely wrinkle free khakis rather uselessly. Where had he....? No. Not there. He didn't think...but maybe....?

"Emmett. *Emmett!*" Cellphone and wallet in hand, chin down and eyebrows raised, she tapped her bare foot against the cool kitchen tile. "You left them in the recliner last night."

"Sorry. I love you. I've got to go. Call you at lunch!" He stuffed the phone and wallet into his pants pockets and tried for a hurried run out the door. On his tall, rather gangly frame it looked more like a repetitive forward lurch.

Zari shook her head and laughed. Absent-minded professor, indeed.

~***~

"Ouch!" Hot, soapy water splashed over her feet. Zari blinked, looking around. *What is happening?* The kitchen was bright, brighter than it should possibly be. Her hands were shaking again, and the sink she'd been filling a few minutes ago had overflowed, leaving puddles on the floor and her braided rug sopping wet. She grabbed towels from the drawer and soaked up the mess from the floor then hung her rug out on the line.

Pouring a cold glass of green tea, Zari tried to settle her nerves. She sat at their kitchen table, sipping her drink with one hand and rearranging patches of fabric with the other, trying out a new quilt idea as blues music belted out of her iPod.

This looks good, I like the purple against the yellow....what is wrong with me? It could be....NO. No, it can't be....that. I won't allow it. I'm happy. I'm so happy, and we are so good together. So normal. I'm normal. I am. I'm not....like them.

A talk with Mr. Grady. That's what she needed.

The sun was bright, the breeze faint, and she was feeling better as she walked along the dirt road. Zari smiled as his house came into view. Three down from her own and on the opposite side of the road, Mr. Grady had been an unexpected blessing when she and Emmett had bought their home. She waved her hand and called out in greeting to the sweet neighbor she'd come to think of as a grandfather. His toffee colored skin, wide, honest brown eyes, and tufts of white hair endeared her heart to him, somehow.

"Baby Girl!" Mr. Grady stood smiling on the weathered old porch, his chair still rocking from the sudden departure of his weight. "How you doin'?"

Rather than answer, she lifted her skirt and hopped up the three stairs in one leap, throwing her arms around him. She squeezed harder, enjoying the scent of him: Old Spice and cherry cough drops.

"Sit, Baby Girl, *sit*. Tell me 'bout what you and that fine husband of yours been up to."

"Oh, you know Mr. Grady. Emmett's taken on a couple extra classes at the university. I've been busy at the market, keeping enough quilts handy for those who want 'em." Zari waved her hand in the air to indicate they'd been overcome with responsibilities.

"Working on that old farmhouse, still?"

"Yeah, yeah. We been working on the, um, back porch these last few days. Keeps us busy." A faint pink tinge appeared on her cheeks.

"Shoo, these old houses, huh? Ain't one thing, it's another. Suntea?" He grinned at her, crows feet crinkling up around his eyes.

"Sure, Mr. Grady. Sounds good."

The old man shuffled into his house, the slightly bent frame of the metal door banging against Zari's seat. Five generations, he'd told her that before. Five generations of his family had lived here. *Will I have any generations after me? What if I can't? Or what if I do, and they're like.....*

"Here y'are. Nice and cold. So tell me what projects you kids got going over at your place? What kind of work you doing on the porch?"

Zari sat straight and cleared her throat. "Well you know, I don't know much about you know, that kind of work, Mr. Grady. I just um, I just sort of hold the tools and Emmett, um, well he tells me what to do with them. I just do what he tells me to."

They rocked in quiet unison. James Grady's kind eyes were watching his German shepherd, Rocko, running in the grass, and Zari's eyes were pained, squinting into the distance, contemplating. Her right hand worked at the peeling white paint of her wooden rocker, and tiny chips gathered near her feet, a pile of dirty snow.

"Mr. Grady?"

"Yes, child."

"Did you ever keep anything from Miss Maylie? I don't mean, like, a *lie*, but just...just not told her something? Because maybe...maybe telling her would hurt her? "

"Yes, yes, I have. And it's not something I'd recommend doing, Baby Girl. Caused a heap of problems. And I ended up hurting her anyways. That husband of yours, he's a good man. You just tell him what's troubling you, and he'll help you with it. I know it. I got faith in him. Maybe girl, maybe you need to have a bit more faith in your man?" He tucked his chin and raised his brows at her, a mild admonishment.

"Maybe. Do you think I...."

"Hush! Listen...you hear that?"

Zari quieted, tuning in to the sounds of nature surrounding them on the lonely road.

The grass crunched softly beneath Rocko's heavy paws.

Somewhere in the distance, a mother called out for her child, a whisper of worry in her voice.

Rocko panted, in and out, in and out.

Boards of the old porch groaned under the burden of their combined weight.

A snake hissed.

A snake?

"Mr. Grady," Zari whispered urgently, "there's a snake near the porch!" Her stomach quivered, sickness boiling up into her throat. Fear pierced her chest, an ice pick of anxiety.

He nodded grimly. "Been a mess of them around here lately. I've shot a few of 'em. Worried Rocko might get bit. Rocko. Rocko! You get up here now, that's it, come on."

The dog loped up the stairs, curling up at his owner's feet. Mr. Grady reached down and patted the head of his faithful companion.

Zari forced herself to breathe. *It's just a snake. It's just a snake.*

"Well Mr. Grady, I think I'll head home now. Won't be long

and Emmett will be home from work. I want to get dinner on."

"All right, Baby Girl. You come back around sometime soon. I'll have Miss Maylie make you up some cookies or somethin'. You remember what I said, right?" He pointed a gnarled, shaking finger at her and raised his eyebrows.

Zari smiled and nodded, turning and heading down the drive.

~***~

"Mama! Mom. Mommy! My tooth came out! My tooth came out!" A tiny Zari held the minuscule white pearl in the air, a symbol of victory, her triumphant, gaping smile shining in an empty room. "Mama!" The small girl with dark blond braids, clad in purple pajamas, started down the hall. She opened the first door, "Mama?"...but it was empty. A small, dimpled hand turned the knob on the second door, and the softly whispered word, "Mama?" echoed again in the emptiness. Trepidation filled her. The sounds emanating from the last room felt frightening. Zari's steps were slow, her little feet shuffling on the olive green carpet, pausing before the partially open door. "Mommy?" Holding her prize before her, she tiptoed into the darkened bedroom and took in Mama's deep red comforter on the floor, stained with...something dark. It looked sticky and she wanted to reach out and touch it. The curtains were drawn, and a stream of sunlight shone through the crack between the window frame and the edge of the fabric. Her young mind attempted to make sense of the scene before her. Mama was on the big bed, head lolling to the side, jaw slack. Her white shoulders were bare —the burgundy sheet barely covering her swollen breasts—and from her eyes shot a white light. It reminded Zari of a bright flashlight. Nan was there with her, head upturned, beams of the same white light shooting from her eyes. Something scary was coming out of Mama's mouth. It

looked like a snake! Scaly, black, and twisting, its writhing form seemed to be dancing, enjoying its slow ascent from the darkness it had been trapped within. "Mommy?" It was less than a whisper now, just her lips forming the word and a breath of hot air. Nan's mouth opened, and before it dove into that dark cavern, the eye of the snake focused on Zari. She stood there, her bones feeling as if they had disappeared, replaced by quivering jelly, yet Zari was riveted. With a quick snap of its head, the twisting black form entered Nan's mouth with a slurping sound as loud as thunder. The tiny white tooth tumbled silently into the carpet. Her breath came in fast, shuddering gasps now; her heartbeat so quick the individual poundings seemed one long, fluid movement. Minutes longer than hours ticked by, Nan's body jerking violently in rhythm to whatever the snake was doing inside of her. At last! The snake withdrew, its head covered in a thick, sickening mucus; the slime dripping onto the sheets. Nan collapsed on the bed; her eyes had lost their light now, and only the whites of her eyes remained. Mama's body began to twist, drawing the snake back inside her, but before it succumbed the serpent turned its wet, disgusting little head toward the corner of the room.

"Zari! You are one of us!"

~***~

"Babe! Zari! Wake up, it's okay, I'm here, ssshhhhh, I'm here."

Zari fought through the tight fog of sleep, the nightmare still vivid before her eyes. Her mouth was open, and she begged her body to allow the scream in her belly to release from her mouth. Her body refused to comply. Snapshots of past and present argued for attention and it was impossible to determine which was reality: Mama's limp, naked form beneath the dark red sheet, Emmett's voice in her ear, Nan's dead white eyes, Emmett's large, strong hands on her shoulders, the snake, the snake, the snake, swarming between the images, a venomous, treacherous hunter.

Emmett stared at Zari, the stark terror on her face causing splinters in his heart. Her beautiful gray-green eyes were frozen, locked onto something he could not see; her sun-kissed skin pasty white; her trembling hands fisting their sheets, her breaths coming in short, painful spurts. The nightmares were coming with frightening frequency now, and his inability to do anything to stop them left Emmett feeling less than impotent. He wrapped his arms around her, pulling her up onto his lap and dipping his head so that his mouth was directly at her ear. "I love you. I love you. I'm here, baby. I'm here. It's okay. You're safe. I'm here, I'm here." The soft murmurings of his tender voice echoed in Zari's mind, shoving past the gruesome visions, the hissing terror. Her heartbeat slowed, her breathing became more normal, and she realized she was moving back and forth, back and forth. Emmett was rocking her, loving her, keeping her safe. Zari blinked, and clarity reigned. She was home, she was *home.* The snake was not here, the only thing coiling around her were Emmett's strong, warm arms. Oh, how she loved him.

"I think you need to see a doctor," Emmett said, his voice firm. Lines of worry settled about his eyes.

"No. No doctors. I'm fine. I'm just…it's just, bad memories from the past, you know? I've just got to get through it. The dreams will settle down, they always have before. Remember right before our wedding? They got worse then, and after a few weeks, they disappeared again. I'll be all right. I've got you." Zari smiled and leaned back on the couch, rubbing Emmett's back with soft, comforting circles.

Elbows on knees and head in his hands, Emmett sighed. "Yeah, but babe, this is way worse than it was back then. And the look on your face during these episodes, the way you shake, you just seem so utterly terrified. I mean it scares me to see you this way. I want to be able to fix it for you."

"The problem with being as smart as you are, love, is that you read too many things, and you know too many things that cause you to freak out and worry over stuff that is absolutely normal. They're just bad dreams, Emmett. I'm fine."

I'm fine. I'm normal. I'm normal.

"No. Listen, I…you know I understand the memories, the trauma. Sometimes, I still have nightmares from my childhood, too. But it's not just the dreams, sweetheart. I mean, the dreams are bad. And if you could see the way you look during them, you'd see why I worry. You look like you're going to *die*, Zari." Emmett pulled her closer, until her head rested on his shoulder, dreads tumbling over his chest and abdomen; the weight of them was somehow comforting. "I've seen you shaking."

Her head snapped up; a flicker of angst crossed her features.

"What do you mean, *shaking*?" she asked, her voice tight.

"You know what I'm talking about. You've been trying to hide it for weeks. Your hands, your arms shake."

"I didn't want to worry you."

"It didn't work," he said, dryly.

"I don't like doctors. I won't go."

"God, you're stubborn! What if you have, I don't know, a

brain tumor or something? "

"I don't have a brain tumor." *Maybe I do. I'd prefer that.*

"But what if you do? I love you." His voice cracked. "I don't want to lose you."

"I'm not going anywhere, Emmett. You're stuck with me, like it or not. And you're going to be late for work. Your hair is a mess, and you've still got on yesterday's clothes. Go in to work like that, and your students will think you've been out all night partying, getting lucky with some hot chick."

"I *am* lucky with some hot chick. They don't make 'em hotter than you, babe." He smiled, finally.

"Come on. I'll pack your lunch. Got your graded papers? Keys? I think I saw your wallet on the floor in the living room. Get hustling, Professor."

Chapter Two

Storm's A-brewin.

*"Now didn't it rain
Rain, rain, children?
Rain
Oh my Lord."*
-Gospel, original artist unknown

Walking in to market, Zari tugged her quilt-laden cases on wheels. Her booth was in a fortunate location near the giant doors, and she set up quickly. Several of her bright, larger quilts hung on racks, and the smaller ones were folded strategically on the three tables that formed her official space. More unique items, like the quilted one-of-a-kind wall hangings, were displayed on specially created racks Emmett had ordered for her from a craftsman in town. Zari moved with precision, her capable, work-roughened hands slipping gracefully from one task to another.

"Zari! Hey girl!"

"Jessa, hey! Let me just….." Zari dropped the few remaining small items into a box, and kicked it under the back table. "…all right. You need help setting up?" Thirty minutes before opening, and Jessa was perpetually running behind. Boxes with beautifully crocheted blankets and shawls spilled haphazardly over the tables, blues and greens dominating the selection but pinks and yellows were plenty as well. Organization was clearly not Jessa's strong suit, but she was talented at her craft and one of the friendliest women Zari had known. Petite and pretty with large, clear blue eyes, long brown hair and pale skin littered with freckles, Jessa was known to draw men to her like flies to honey. She was slightly overweight and had a persistent pink flush to her cheeks that lent her the look of a robust farm girl. Fiercely protective of friends and family, Jessa was precious to Zari in so many ways. Laughing, the two friends set to work getting Jessa's work out on display.

"This goes here?" Zari questioned.

"No…no, that one goes up on the rack." Jessa pointed to an oddly shaped wooden configuration on the table.

"You can't be so picky, girl, we only have ten minutes."

"I know, I know. But next week, next week I'm going to be more organized, I swear. Hand to heart."

"Of course. You always are." Zari's tone called her bluff.

Jessa popped Zari on the shoulder with an empty cardboard box. "Right, and you're Miss Perfection, aren't you?"

"Absolutely." Zari curtsied, lifting her long skirt high on the sides. "Miss Perfection, at your service, ma'am."

"Oh, stop. You aren't so perfect, and you know it. But I'll tell you who *is* perfect, is that hot husband of yours. Mmmnn. " Waving a hand in front of her face to indicate Emmett's level of heat, and rounding her eyes until she resembled a moonstruck teenager, Jessa continued, "Lucky thing you found him first, or I'da snapped him up like *that.*"

Zari giggled, then sobered, thinking of her sexy, kind, and thoughtful husband. Sweet Emmett. "You're right. He is perfect. *And* hot. I'm a lucky girl, and I know it."

"Don't you forget it, girl."

"Looks like you're set up pretty good here, I'm heading back over to my little hole in the wall."

Three, two, one... the giant doors swung open, and the zombie horde of shoppers piled in. Old men in overalls dragged along by enthusiastic wives in wildly colored pantsuits with sensible shoes and fat purses, bored teenagers, and little kids with hands that seemed simultaneously everywhere filled the small aisles between crafters.

"This one for sale?" Zari blinked at the middle-aged woman dressed in neon green —from her huge floppy hat to her incredibly high heels— and wondered at the absurdity of the question.

No, lady, I just pay for my space here so I can drag my months of hard work in and not sell it.

"Yes, ma'am!" she answered brightly instead. "The price is on the tag there, interested? "

Boxing the quilt up for the woman she'd mentally named Kermit, Zari kept watch on the overly touchy-feely kid at the opposite end of the table. One baby blanket on the floor by her shiny Mary Janes and two more in her hands, the impeccably dressed little girl did not appear to have a parent nearby.

"Here you are, and thanks for shopping at Hippie Quilts!" Zari handed the boxed-up quilt for Kermit over the table and smiled, tucking her newly acquired cash into her satchel. Slipping down to the other end of the table, she spoke kindly to the child who was still pulling Zari's small quilts off and onto the floor. "Sweetie? I work hard to make these blankets, please don't drop them on the floor. They'll get dirty." Zari bent to pick them up from the floor and shake the light dusting of dirt off.

The child burst into tears.

Zari was alarmed.

"I can't find my mama! I want my mama!" the little girl wailed.

"It's okay, it's okay. Come here, we'll find your mom." Pulling her phone from the satchel, Zari explained, "I can call someone to page your mom. Tell me your name, and market security will help us. Just calm down, sweetheart."

"Kayde. My name is Kayde. I just want my mommy." Her broken, hiccupping voice and shuddering shoulders pierced Zari's heart, and she knelt to wrap her arms around Kayde, drawing the child close to her chest. Sniffling, the girl pulled back and looked Zari directly in the face. *What mesmerizing, golden eyes this kid has.* Unable to break her gaze, Zari continued to stare. Kayde's head turned at an odd angle, and when she spoke, her voice was suddenly loud and tinny.

"Zari, you are one of us!" Robotically, the child's mouth moved.

No, no, no, this isn't happening.

"You cannot escape who you are!"

"I'm *not*. I'm not like that. I won't be." Involuntarily, Zari shivered.

"We will come for you. You cannot escape." Kayde's mouth opened and shut like a marionette, her eyes swirling pools of hypnotic caramel.

How is this happening?

"YOU. ARE. SLITHER."

"I am NOT. Just go away! I don't want to be this." Zari's mind was filled with an overwhelming desire to run, but her legs didn't seem to share the motivation.

"We are all connected. You belong to us. We are coming."

Please wake up, please wake up, please wake up.

Realizing her voice was becoming shrill, Zari fought to bring it down to a fierce whisper.

"Please, just leave me alone." She was pleading now, crying.

"The serpent must feed."

Teeth chattering and body shuddering, Zari wrapped her arms tightly around herself, willing the scene to disappear, willing it to never have happened, willing her body to wake up home in bed with Emmett's sweet face asleep on the pillow across from hers. She shut her eyes, hard, wishing she had a pair of ruby slippers to click herself away from this mess. The entire Lollipop Guild would be preferable to this terrifying little girl.

"Zari!"

Her eyes snapped open.

The child's face twisted, contorting like putty in the hands of a toddler. One eye drooped, the nose slid to the side, the mouth opened impossibly wide and directly in front of Zari's face.

Zari's breath froze in her chest. Her heartbeat slowed, her muscles melted within her like hot candle wax, and her eyes were involuntarily transfixed on Kayde's monstrous features. In abject horror, Zari watched as the bulge that began in Kayde's chest grew fatter, slithering into the child's small, pale neck and emerging from the throat. Entranced, she stared into the cavern of Kayde's dark, open mouth and the black snake rose, scaly and slime-covered, over the small pink tongue, past the teeth, out through the lips. *Not possible. Not possible. This cannot be real.* Zari gasped, attempting to move some air into her lungs, but her chest was still a block of ice. Dizzy from the lack of oxygen, yet still unable to move, Zari's mind swam in confusion. It was *right there.* The serpent hovered near her neck, then moved up, up, up to her chin, hissing near her mouth, past her nose and finally resting just inches from her eyes. *Air. I need air.*

Its mouth opened, the forked tongue slipping in and out, in and out. The deep, robotic voice of the snake would haunt her dreams, her soul, she knew it.

"Zari. We are coming. You cannot escape."

Kayde began to evaporate, disappearing pixels in a world that was suddenly black and white. Shiny black patent leather Mary Janes and ruffled socks were the first to go, followed by the slow dissolution of chubby, childish legs. The flowered hem of her dress blew away, bit by bit, until all that remained of the little girl were dangling arms and her still-tilted head, two perfectly coiled black braids dropping past her chin, settled on dead air. Kayde blinked, and her eyes became dark, thick pits of slime. Desperate for a solid breath, Zari gasped again, pounding her chest in an effort to send her lungs into action. The face of the child was contorting again, a melted appearance that left the cheeks and jaw stretched further, color deepening to the shade of soot, and the head of the snake disintegrated to ash. Disgust and fear disguised as bile rose from deep in Zari's gut, heated rivulets burning upward through the ice block in her chest. The sudden ability to inhale startled her to near collapse, and she reached out reflexively to grab onto the table. The first breath out was a long, static-like wheeze. **BAM!** The double doors slammed open, a fierce, visible wind gusted in to the market place, steering itself around chairs, tables, and frozen-in-time people, slowing as it neared Zari and what was left of Kayde. Funneling itself into a swirling chasm, the wind began to suck chunks of the hovering face away, gobbling it up as bits of blackened spittle dripped onto the smooth cement floor. Pieces of shoulder were torn away, exposing rotting muscle and grisly yellow fat beneath. Inch by inch, what remained of the arms were siphoned up into the chasm, until only the right hand was unclaimed. Zari continued to gulp air, drunk on oxygen, her peaked skin slowly returning to the color that spoke of long days working in the sun. *Emmett, Emmett, Emmett. I just want Emmett. I want his strong, safe arms around me, making this stop.* She drifted for a moment, imagining leaning in to his warm, solid frame, his steady heartbeat echoing in her ear. The lone, dimpled hand fashioned itself into a fist, the first finger creeping out, unfolding to a point. A familiar voice resounded in her mind, and Zari found it impossible to reconcile the voice with the disembodied hand. Crackling like old radio static, yet balmy and soothing as honey, the voice of the man she loved like family was inside her, surrounding her, filling the eerily silent market from rafters to cement:

"Don't you forget what I said now, Baby Girl."

Sickening laughter rained down on Zari, furious and frightening; a hailstorm of emotion pelting her skin. Immediately, her spine chilled and a *whoosh* passed through her body, stealing her breath once again. The hand was gone, the funnel sealed, and color began to seep back into the scene around her. A tinkling sound caught her attention, and her head shot around to locate the cause. A glimmer on the ground, just a step away, and she bent to grasp the tiny object between forefinger and thumb.

A minuscule white pearl.

My tooth.

~***~

Simultaneously chilled and sweating, Zari remained crouched on the floor, watching as people began moving again, painfully slow and arthritic motions as they creaked to life. Color seeped back into her surroundings, and muffled voices rose in alarm. Frantic bits of sentences sailed through the air:
"What *was* that?" A man's voice, confused in the chaos.

"A tornado!" A woman, hysterical, the words were followed by shrieking, and Zari imagined the faceless woman was wringing her hands.

"Is it over?" Another male, a teenager guessing from the high-pitched crack in his voice.

"Get down! Get down!" Deep-voiced, a different woman took command.

The mess left in the wake of the great wind was evident: overturned tables, merchandise strewn about the floor, crying children with runny noses and whimpering women turning to their men for explanation. This oddly belated reaction appeared bizarre to Zari, but she supposed the human mind had to somehow compensate for the inexplicable. She scooted beneath one of her tables nearest the wall, hoping to fit in with the others scrambling for shelter as she continued to take deep breaths and work to still the shaking deep within her. Her thoughts were jumbled, piling one atop another as she fought for calm. Clamping her teeth together in an effort to still the chatter, Zari closed her eyes and tried to focus. *I am not...I am NOT what she said I am. I would never, never DO the things they do. I would never feed off...anyone. Disgusting. But she said they were coming. What if...? What if it's at my house? Emmett! What if they hurt him? I've got to go home.* She crawled out from under the table, standing up slowly with her hand pressed in to the arch of her back.

"Jess? Jessa! Are you all right?"

"Yeah. I think so. Are you okay? Wasn't that weird?"

"Yeah. Hey, I need to go home. I want to...um, check on Emmett. I'll come back for my stuff later, okay?"

Jessa opened her mouth to reply, then shut it. Zari was already gone.

~***~

"Emmett! Emmett? Where are you, babe?" She knew he was home. His rusted old truck was in the drive, but he wasn't in any of the downstairs rooms. Trepidation formed a lump in her throat and saliva pooled in her cheeks as she gripped the rail and started up the stairs on shaky legs. She'd run the three miles home from the market, and her muscles were staging a protest. "Hon? You home?" Zari turned on the hardwood landing at the top of the stairs, squeezing her eyes shut as she faced their closed bedroom door. "Em...." Opening the door, she stopped and stared. Fully dressed, Emmett lay sprawled across their bed atop the king-sized quilt done in burgundy and various shades of green that she'd made with her own hands. Scuffed brown shoes still on, wrinkled khakis, half-untucked light blue dress shirt with the top three buttons undone, and his wireframe glasses tilted at an awkward angle on his face. His thin frame was so still. Frighteningly so. Was he breathing? Her heart caught an odd beat. *Please be okay please be okay please be okay...* tiptoeing into the bedroom, Zari fought images from her childhood as the scene before her changed from present to past and back again. *Her mother. The snake.* Emmett. Dear, sweet Emmett. *The shag carpet of her mother's bedroom.* The cold hardwood beneath her feet in the room she shared with her husband. *They said her mother was weak from a difficult pregnancy. She'd needed strength, and Nan allowed the feeding.* Light green cotton curtains in the window. *An act of love, they'd told her, attempting to explain away the horror she'd witnessed. Nan had been left ill from it herself, Zari remembered.* Emmett's grandfather's sword, resting on the rack mounted above their bed. The only piece of his childhood he'd held onto, all these years. *She'd stayed in bed for a month or more, and Zari had been made to take food each day to the grandmother she could no longer look in the eye. She'd found this part of her lineage revolting, and never had been able to look on her little sister with anything close to love.* But this was now, and the only person who mattered was Emmett. If they'd hurt him or...or worse...Zari had reached their bed and climbed in, sitting on her knees and clasping his face in her hands. "Emmett? EMMETT! ANSWER ME!" His eyes snapped open, dark blue pools confused by abrupt awakening, his brows furrowed. He sat up quickly, grabbing Zari's wrists as he did. Emmett's sharp intake of breath was audible in the quiet room, and he blinked rapidly, grappling with the thick web of sleep that still held a good portion of his mind hostage. "What is it? What's wrong?" His voice was low and urgent; even half asleep the desire to protect Zari was his first thought. Relieved, Zari held him against her chest, laughing. "You're okay?"

"I...I think so. Should I not be?" He blinked rapidly,

dragging the rest of his mind awake and looking down her shirt. *Gorgeous.* "But I'm definitely better now."

"I was just kind of worried. You looked so still it…I mean it didn't look like you were breathing. It scared me." Her right hand slid into his curls, his hair sifting through her fingers like sand. "I love you so much."

"No worries, babe. I'm breathing." The sleepiness was disappearing from his voice, and he sounded absolutely awake.

"Yeah. Down my shirt." Her skin was tingling in response to the tickle of his breath.

"Do I have to stop?"

"Absolutely not. What were you doing napping up here, anyway? You that exhausted from perfect participles and semicolons, Professor?"

"Ugh, you don't even know, babe. I've had my students in review all this week, getting ready for finals. They're exhausting. Sometimes I'm not sure if I'm teaching college or kindergarten."

"That bad, huh?" She wasn't unsympathetic.

"Worse. But you're making me feel so much better!"

"You mean my boobs are making you feel so much better?" His breath was hot on her breasts; the moist warmth of it comforting.

"Maybe. I can't help it. I like them." The tips of his ears gained a faint pinkish tint.

Zari laughed again, the horrifying little girl from earlier

slowly drifting from memory. She could almost, *almost* pretend Kayde wasn't even real.

But not quite.

She bent to kiss the top of Emmett's head, then his forehead, his nose, his mouth. She was suddenly on fire as she shoved his shoulders back down on the bed, leaning over him and covering his wrists with her hands. Zari's breath was ragged as she brought her mouth to his again, enjoying the feeling of his body arching against hers. He was strong enough to lift her smaller frame up. He tossed her grip from his wrists as easily as the wind could pluck a dried leaf from a limb, flipping Zari onto her back as if her weight was insignificant. His hands —how she loved his hands: large, strong, and firm— were at once raking across her body and tangled in her dreads, driving the temperature between them up to what was nearly an unbearable level. Their kiss grew deeper, and the heat of his breath left a chill across her tongue, then a shiver down her spine. Zari yanked her shirt up over her head, and she watched as desire lit those dark blue eyes with a furious pleasure. The slow grin that spread across Emmett's face lent a heaviness to his features that Zari recognized, and responded to with aching excitement deep in her gut and a low gasp of wanting. Closing her eyes, she focused on feeling every place his hands touched, every bit of skin his breath grazed, the chilling, burning sensation that remained each time his lips left her body. Slipping her hands up inside his shirt, the feel of his bare skin against her own was nearly her undoing. Zari fumbled with his buttons, her fingers shaking with desire. Few things felt so satisfying as sliding Emmett's shirt off his shoulders, and she was pleased, as she was every time, at the knowledge his body belonged to her alone.

She made love to him to remember.

She made love to him to forget.

And she made love to him again.

It was late, and Zari batted some errant dreads from her face, squinting her eyes against the evening sun shining in through their window. She pulled Emmett closer, using her arm to draw his body nearer to hers and smiled. His head settled in the crook of her shoulder, fitting into the groove as if it had been carved for him alone. Closing her eyes, she used her fingers to trace the outlines of tattoos and scars she knew were there: the map of his back, his journey, she knew it as well as she knew the palm of her own hand. *Six*: six freckles, one cluster of four near his right shoulder blade and a set of twins near his left hip; *three*: three tattoos, each an image with a line of explanation next to it; *thirteen*: thirteen pitted circles in a straight line down his spine, a reminder of the times his mother's boyfriend had used him as an ashtray. The jagged lash marks across Emmett's lower back that ran hip to hip were more difficult to count; the scars where the tender, childish flesh had once been ripped open by the same man and his whip were so layered that they appeared innumerable.

The toughened, raised skin that had healed over the original injuries was a testimony about the man she shared her life with.

"Mmmmm…you are amazing, babe." His large hand rested languidly on her breast.

"Sorry. Didn't mean to wake you up."

"It's okay. I need to get up. Got work to do. But I wish I could just stay here, getting more of what you gave me earlier." He gently squeezed the mound of flesh in his hand.

"Yeah? You liked that, huh?" She was teasing him, letting

her fingers drift lightly up and down his arm, feeling the gooseflesh as it erupted.

"*Liked* it? Babe, you blew my mind." Zari grinned. Emmett rubbed his face, sitting up against the headboard and running his hands through his hair. Beneath the sheets, Zari's sweat-dampened leg was still tangled in his.

"Hand me my glasses?"

Zari's free hand groped around the nightstand, finally landing on his wire frames. Holding them just a bit too far away, she leaned over and kissed him again. "I love the way you make me feel."

"Zari! I can't do this again…not that I don't want to…I do, actually…but I'm so far behind on work. I've got to get up." She felt a firmness pressing against her hip, confirming that he did, truly, want more. "But, you too. I mean, the way you make me feel. You drive me crazy, babe. "

"Getting up?" She wished he wouldn't. She felt safe and contented in his arms.

"Five more minutes. Hey, what were you doing home so early today, anyway? Everything okay?"

"Yeah. There was this bad storm over by the market." *Technically true.* "I was worried it hit over here, so I ran home. I'll run back over tomorrow to get my car and pack up my things if Jessa didn't already do it for me."

"You *ran* home. Immediately after a bad storm. You thinking straight today, or what?" His voice was softly scolding.

"Okay, yeah, probably not my smartest move. But I was

worried about you. I just wanted to make sure you were safe." Zari's hand drifted across his chest, pausing a moment to play with the springy, curly hair that populated the region.

"Next time though, you know. I want you to be safe, too. Think it through, babe." His arm clenched tighter around her, smashing her cheek flat against his chest.

"Aren't you glad I came home early, though? Considering...." Using a finger, she traced a circle around his nipple.

"My God. Yes! You make me crazy. And as an added bonus, you got my mind off this insane dream I was having when you woke me up." An attractive rose blush tinted his cheeks.

"Bad dream, huh. What was it about?" Zari narrowed down the circle, closer and closer to the center, until...*bingo.*

Emmett started and coughed. "It was about snakes. They were everywhere."

~***~

I have to tell him. I can't. I have to. I have to. What would I say? 'Hey babe, guess what? You've married a freakish snake girl! Here's to hoping I don't accidentally kill you!' Holy hell. I can't do this. But he should be prepared. What if they come for him? What if they hurt him? What if I hurt him? No. I would never hurt Emmett. Not on purpose. But they might. He needs to know.

Zari stood in their bedroom, resolute. She knew the path she needed to follow. She had to tell him the truth, and she had to do it now. He would leave. She knew he was going to leave her. A hollow ache in her heart had already begun, carving out a place for her loneliness to rest. She dressed, thinking this could be the last time Emmett's clothes would lay on the floor of their shared room. Staring, Zari took in the scattered, wrinkled heaps of jeans and dress shirts that never made it to the basket. It drove her crazy, his messiness. She knelt on the floor, picking a faded green button-down up in her hands and smelling it. *Emmett.* Zari crawled back onto their bed, placing her body directly over Emmett's usual sleeping space. Closing her eyes, she tried to remember exactly how her husband had lain after they'd made love. Had his leg been bent, like that? And his left arm, it had reached across her pillow, under her neck. She moved her left arm accordingly. Somehow, Zari could feel his presence: his warmth, his scent, his body. *Remember this. Remember him. Oh, Emmett.*

The staircase was so long. For each step she took there seemed another four at the bottom. Perhaps it was never ending and this conversation wouldn't have to take place. An irrational thought, but a balm nonetheless. Right hand on the scuffed wooden rail, Zari straightened her shoulders. She hiccupped, and it caught in her chest. Her left hand rose, hesitantly, toward the pain, and her cold fingers came to rest just above her breasts, pressing into her skin, leaving temporary white indentations. Eyes focused on the landing, the air before her was distorted, the way it is when one peers through the smoke of a fire on a hot summer night. With each step, dread settled into her being with a weary heaviness.

Emmett was sitting in his chair, elbows on his knees, pinching the bridge of his nose with his thumb and forefinger. Papers were spread out in piles in front of him: on the hardwood floor, on the banged up, second-hand coffee table, on the arms of the recliner, on his lap. Books and binders were fanned out in a stack on the floor to the right of him. His shirt was unbuttoned, and his feet were bare. The awkward length of his hair had curls winging out above his ears. Zari stood in their living room, burning the precious sight of him into her memory. She attempted to swallow, but the dryness of her throat stopped it midway, leaving a hard, painful lump near her tonsils. One more. She just wanted one more day. Minute. Hour. Kiss.

"Babe? Emmett? Could we talk for a minute?" His bloodshot eyes looked up at her, and he smiled.

"Sure, hon. I need a break, anyway." She walked toward him, each step a deliberate, forced action. Zari gingerly placed her feet where the hardwood peeked through the edges of papers, sitting down on the couch. She held her hand out, "Come sit with me." His hands—oh! How she loved those hands—shuffled the paper stacks into some sort of organized disarray and set them carefully on the floor to the left of his chair. Zari watched as he stood and stretched, his khakis hiking up above his ankles as he reached his arms toward the ceiling. Emmett bent back, fist digging into his tailbone. Straightening, he closed the distance between his recliner and the plush green couch with one long step. Zari reached up, guiding his lanky frame down so his head rested on her lap. He looked up at her, a drowsy grin spreading across his face. An ache filled her at the sight of his crooked tooth. She resisted an odd desire to reach up and touch it with her finger. A pain in her chest caught her breath and she pressed her hand against his cheek. "You've been working too hard." Tenderness softened her eyes, and she blinked rapidly as she dropped her head close to his face. "I love you, Emmett. I've loved you since the day I met you. You know that, right?" Zari bent closer until her lips met his, and he responded with a fervor that belied his obvious fatigue. Heated excitement rose from her belly, and Zari fought to hold it in, saving it within herself so she would never forget the effect Emmett's body had on hers. *Remember this. Remember him.* He brushed some hair back from her face and broke their kiss.

"Aw, babe. I know. I love you, too." Emmett brought her hand down to rest on the left side of his chest, speaking earnestly. "You've always belonged to me. Right here. You always will." Zari turned her hand so it clasped his. *I wish that were true.* She took a deep breath. "Emmett, I…I…need to make you dinner." The words came out in a rush. Drops of sweat broke out on her forehead and the back of her neck. She felt a familiar tremor moving down her wrists. "You…we haven't eaten today. What sounds good?" He laughed and sat up, running his hands through his hair, leaving the already messy curls sticking out at random angles. "Zari, your hands are shaking again." Emmett held her quivering hands in his strong, warm ones. His voice turned serious. "You need to see a doctor. This isn't right." A strangled sound erupted from her throat, part laugh, part cough. "I'm okay."

"No. No, you are not."

"Tacos? Rice?" *Deflect. Deflect.*

"I'm serious, Zari." There was an edge in his voice.

"So am I. I'm starving." *No going back now.*

"Zari." The edge was sharper now. Zari could almost see the blade of it, glistening.

"Soup and grilled cheese." *I might be a bit safer in the kitchen.*

"Zari!" The two syllables of her name bit through the air, slicing.

"Emmett!" *Time to go.*

The pink in his otherwise pale cheeks was attractive, no doubt, but Zari recognized the fire in his eyes and knew this had gone beyond teasing. She stood quickly, walking toward the kitchen without another word.

Where is it? It's somewhere in here. I remember buying it...if my hands weren't so shaky. She rummaged through the cabinets, looking for the can she wanted. "Hey!" Zari squealed and stood on her tiptoes as large, strong hands settled on her hips. "I was looking for....oh wait. I found it." The can of chicken-free chicken noodle soup tumbled onto the counter, then to the floor with a loud bang after the sudden twitch in her wrist made her drop it.

"Let me help." Emmett bent and picked the can up from the floor.

"I've got it." Zari reached out, digging into his hand for the can, clamping her fingers around the metal cylinder.

"I want to help you. Let me help." His hand, so much bigger than hers, curled tight around her fingers.

"Emmett, I'm cap..." Chin up, her eyes lit with fire, Zari struggled to yank the soup can—and her hand—from his grasp.

"Yes. You are capable. And you are fine, more than fine. I know. But let me help." His tone was patient but firm, and his other hand was resting on the small of her back. He pulled her closer.

"But I can..." She broke off, gritting her teeth.

"Woman! You're my wife. I'm your husband. I *want* to help you." Frustration lined his face; he pressed his lips together until they blanched.

"Whatever. I'll make the soup, then." Zari huffed. Actually huffed.

"And I'll get the sandwiches." Emmett grinned, victorious.

Cross-legged they sat, each on one end of the couch. Zari balanced the plate with her sandwich on one knee, and held the bowl of soup in her hand, blowing on a spoonful of noodles and broth.

BAM! BAM! BAM! The unexpected pounding on their front door startled Zari and she dropped her bowl. Spilled hot soup burned her leg through the thin fabric of her skirt. "Ow! Crap…who…?" She leaned forward and gently placed her bowl and plate on the coffee table, mopping up broth from her leg and the couch with the dry parts of her skirt.

Emmett stood. "I've got it." A peek through the gingham door curtain revealed a disheveled Mr. Grady and Miss Maylie, Rocko in tow with his ears down and one front paw scratching at the air. Opening the door, Emmett said, "Everything okay? Come in, come in." Gripping the dog's leash in one hand, and steadying the other against his frail wife's bent back, Mr. Grady and his crew shuffled inside.

"Didn't you hear? Got a storm comin'. Big one. Seen it on the news, said to take cover. We ain't got a basement, and you kids said…"

"Yeah sure. No, you're fine. Let me just carry some chairs downstairs for us to sit on. Zari, check the local news, would you, hon?"

No sooner had she clicked the television on, than the warning sirens began to wail.

The balding weatherman appeared more excited than appropriate, given the seriousness of the situation as he pointed at the dark parts of the map that indicated severe weather was approaching. " ....and if you're within a five-mile radius of this cluster *here*, take cover immediately in a basement or solid center room. If you're in a trailer, please get out and seek shelter! One hundred mile-an-hour winds and orange-size hail expected with probable tornadoes!" he said with a cheery grin. Emmett and Zari's eyes met.

"I'll grab some pillows and blankets. Looks like we might be downstairs for a while," Zari said, moving quickly toward the linen closet.

Emmett easily lifted a kitchen chair on each arm and opened the basement door. "Probably should grab some candles and lighters, too, hon. Just in case." His steps were fast and sure as he hustled down the stairs.

Mr. Grady wrapped one arm around his wife and held tight to the railing as they began their descent. Step, stop. Step, stop. Zari stood behind them, holding a stack of blankets and Rocko's leash. The big dog whined in concern at the unusual events, but complied when Zari whispered, "Sit." Watching the shaky movements of the elderly couple, Zari's eyes misted and she bent her head to wipe them on an edge of the top blanket. That was how she'd always pictured her and Emmett, loving each other, depending on one another, even as the years changed their appearance. He'd be bald and scrawny and she'd be wrinkled and plump and still they'd know the moon and stars rose and set with the love they'd chosen. She blinked rapidly and swallowed hard, and finally started down the stairs. Emmett was on his way back up for chairs, and as he passed Zari and Rocko on the steps, he stopped to cup his hand around the side of her head, drawing her toward his chest. "Love you." He kissed her forehead and continued on his quest.

Zari was unfolding the blankets, wrapping one around Miss Maylie's trembling shoulders, and settled several on the floor. BAM! BAM! BAM! "Who in the...now what?" she muttered, and listened as Emmett's heavy footsteps fell across the floor above her head. Squinting her eyes as if it would help her hear better, she heard her husband conversing with a high-pitched, female voice that seemed remotely familiar. "I'll be right back," she said, and took the stairs a couple at a time. "Emm...oh, hey Jessa!" Her friend was drenched and shivering, making her already petite frame seem even smaller.

"H-h-hey, Zari." Jessa offered a weak smile. "I boxed up your quilts and things, thought I'd drop them by on my way home. Next thing I know, the trees were bending over in the wind, and the sirens were going off. I knew you guys had a basement, so I..." her voice trailed off.

"Yeah, yeah. That's fine! Come on in, we have plenty of room. I'll get you some towels to dry off with. You head on down to the basement. Mr. Grady and his wife are already down there." Zari turned to head up to the bathroom closet, crossing her arms over her chest as she did. The house was warm, but the darkening skies and wailing sirens lent an air of foreboding that left her chilled. She moved her shoulders up and inward, an involuntary action of self-protection. Emmett leaned out the front door, turning his head left then right, wrinkling his brows against the boisterous wind and twisting clouds. "It's getting bad out here," he whispered to no one. A deluge of sideways rain pelted the porch, splattering against Emmett's glasses, leaving streaks. The storm door fought against his strength as he pulled it shut, a billowing gust rounding the thin metal frame away from him. Veins rippled his biceps and he struggled, finally latching the handle and slamming the heavy wooden door closed behind it. Swiftly, Emmett bolted the locks and blew out a breath, as if the howling storm could understand his household was now out of reach. His long back leaned with relief against the door, pressing his shoulders against the painted yellow wood. Removing water-stained glasses from his face, Emmett rubbed the lenses with a corner of his wrinkled blue shirt, then ran a hand through his curls.

The force of the slamming door rattled loose the wreath Zari had made when they'd first moved in to the farmhouse. Burgundy, green, and blue flowers twisted with baby's breath and ribbons were woven through twigs, and the pretty circle dropped from its nail, trapped between the two doors, shuddering against the repetitive, blasting weight of the wind.

Flashlights, batteries, candles, and lighters lined the small table near the makeshift camp the group had made in the basement. A box of crackers was tipped on its side next to a case of bottled water. Electricity was still on, but the lights had flickered several times. The first three times it happened, Miss Maylie had shrieked like she'd sat on a mound of fire ants, but at this point she seemed to be taking the blinking bulbs in stride. Jessa's long hair was still damp, as were her clothes. Wrapped in a heavy fleece blanket and teeth chattering, she was discussing the remainder of the market day with Zari, who was sitting cross-legged on the floor with her skirt tucked under her legs.
"So then, I had this weirdo lady dressed in lime green, like seriously, from hat to heels..."

"Shut *up*! I know that lady! She was at my booth buying a quilt today. I kept calling her 'Kermit' in my head."

"Kermit? Like the frog! That's freakin' awesome, dude. " Jessa squealed with laughter, covering her mouth as she did so as if it would lower the pitch of her voice.

"I know, right? I felt sorry for her poor husband…"

"Zari," Jessa interrupted, leaning over to pick something off her friend's skirt, "something's spilled all over you. Is that…a noodle?" Jessa made a sickly face as the pale, flabby pasta dangled from the pinch of her thumb and forefinger.

Looking down, she replied, "Yeah. I spilled hot soup on myself earlier. It's been so crazy I forgot to change. But I might have something clean in the dryer. Lemme go look."

Springing to her feet, Zari rose from the ground in one fluid motion. Across the room, Miss Maylie watched her with an expression akin to wistfulness, and opened a hand toward Zari – why, she didn't know, but she smiled at the older woman anyway.

"Babe," Emmett began, "why don't you check to see if you've got something dry for Jessa to change into? Her clothes are still pretty wet."

Both girls dissolved into giggles. "Hon, Jessa is barely five feet tall. I'm at least ten inches taller and bigger built. What clothes of mine do you really think will fit her?"

"Well I, I mean, I don't know. Just trying to help." He looked sheepish, and ducked his head. Zari caught his hand and slipped her fingers through his. "I know, babe. I know." She appreciated his misguided effort. Emmett could barely keep himself dressed, what did he know about women's clothes?

Bending down and peeking into the dryer, Zari rummaged through the pile of clothes until she located the one pair of pajama bottoms she'd found that were long enough for her body. "Nobody come in here, I'm changing!" she called out. Allowing her skirt to puddle on the floor and balancing on one leg, Zari hopped around as she slid one foot into her pajama bottoms. Given the situation, the thunder clap shouldn't have been unexpected, but it was. The **BOOM!** was so great, the shaking of the farmhouse could be felt in the concrete of the basement floor. Miss Maylie screamed. Emmett swore. Rocko howled.

Startled, Zari fell backward on the utility room floor, whacking her head on the wall on her way down. Her right arm flung forward and to the side, hitting a table holding several jugs of laundry detergent. The oft-repaired, wobbly leg of the second-hand table collapsed, sending the heavy white bottles tumbling to the floor. Two landed on Zari, and she groaned. The door whipped open. Emmett and Jessa rushed in to find a half-naked Zari lying with one leg partially in her pants and the other leg bare and sticky with the clear liquid dripping from the cracked cap of the laundry soap. The broken table lay precariously near her head, and her long, magnificent dreads were splayed haphazardly across the floor. Zari clutched her head with her hands, whimpering. Emmett was in the room and by her side in seconds, cradling her head in his lap and checking her thoroughly for deep gashes. "There's blood. Let me…sshh, hold still. Just let me find where it's coming from." His thumb traced her hairline, down near her ear and held the few bloody dreads in his hand. "I can't…oh, there it is. Right above your ear, it's cut. And there's a big lump, right in the back of your head." Reaching back, he rifled in the still open dryer and found a hand towel. Dabbing it on the oozing gash, he hummed to his wife as the thunder continued to crash around them. Through the storm, a different pounding sounded, almost too faint to be heard. BAM! BAM! BAM!

"What is that?" Zari put a finger to her lips, encouraging Emmett to quiet down and listen. His voice stilled, leaving a void in the room that seemed immediately filled with a flash of lightning. "I thought I heard…yes! Did you hear that? I think someone's knocking on the door." Zari moved to sit up, blinking against both the pain in her head and the iridescent blue streak of light exploding throughout the basement.

"Just stay still. You're hurt, babe." Emmett's hand hovered a few inches in the air above Zari's midsection, as if he thought he could do anything to hinder his wife's stubborn spirit. She brushed his hand away as she stood.

"Emmett. I can't ignore it. What if someone is hurt?" She held her right hand against the wall to steady herself, allowing her sense of balance to even out as she yanked her pajama bottoms up with her left.

"I'll go with you, then. " He walked behind her on the stairs, watching—but not mentioning—her slightly unsteady gait. The banging on the door was growing persistently louder, and a frantic female voice called out, "Please! Please let us in. I have a child with me! *Please!*" Zari looked back at Emmett briefly, her eyes asking if he recognized the sound of the screaming woman. He shook his head. "Let me open the door." Zari rolled her eyes. "It could be anyone, you know? Just let me…be the man, here." *As if I could turn you into a woman by opening the door?* She grinned, but stood back to preserve his manhood as Emmett turned the knob and peered out on the porch, one arm held back in an effort to protect his helpless, five-foot-ten wife from potential Boogeymen. Zari's shoulders shook with silent laughter. "Hello? Hello?"

A young woman—perhaps twenty years of age, give or take a minute—scrambled awkwardly from where she'd been crouched against the front of the house. Her face was small and pale, with deep-set, wide gray eyes. Straight, white-blond hair hung limp, clumps of it sticking to her nose and lips. A washed-out pink T-shirt clung to her child-sized frame. Thin arms that seemed too small to hold the wiggling, whimpering bundle beneath a fuchsia blanket tightened around their load. "Hi, my um, car broke down out here…" she jerked her head toward the empty road, "…and this is the closest house I saw with lights on. Please, could we come in? I'm scared to stay in my car with this storm. It's so bad out here…" As she spoke, a resounding clap of thunder coupled with a strike of lightning clattered around them. A sickening **THWACK!** shook the farmhouse as a nearby tree split, half of it landing in the street and taking out a power line as it dropped, the other half landing in Zari and Emmett's yard. The house was utterly, absolutely black. "Oh my God!" the young woman shrieked, her hand immediately clasping about her child's head. Emmett reached out immediately and looped his arm around her shoulders, drawing her in from the storm as he spoke. From the basement, Miss Maylie could be heard screaming at the top of her lungs. Rocko was barking, each *woof* louder than the last.

"I'm Emmett, and my wife, Zari, is standing right here…well, somewhere."

"I'm right here, Emmett," she said from behind him. "We have a basement. You are welcome to wait out the storm with us. Despite what you might be hearing, we aren't killing anyone downstairs. Our elderly neighbors are down there, and the wife can be a bit…high-strung."

"I'm, I'm Livvie." Her teeth chattered in the darkness. "I just, I didn't know what else to do." A slight sob escaped her lips. "I thought we were going to die out there."

"You're okay now. It's okay. You're safe." Emmett stated the words firmly, so Livvie would calm down. He reached out until his hand collided with Zari, and he felt her shoulder, her collarbone, her…*oh hey!*"Emmett!" she scolded.

"Sorry. I just wanted to get ahold of your hand, so I knew we were all walking toward the stairs."

"My hand. Mmmhhmmn. Sure, buddy."

"I was! Hey, Livvie? We'll just all keep walking forward, small steps. We've got flashlights and candles downstairs, okay?"

Outside, hail the size of golf-balls was interrupting the steady sheets of rain. The scream of the sirens was barely audible above the howl of the wind. Livvie's arrival had set free the lodged wreath from the front door, and it tumbled in the blackened air across the porch and down three steps. Lying in the rain-bent grass, the pummel of hail smashed the flowers, tearing the petals away from the circle of twigs that had once marked the entrance of Emmett and Zari's happy home.

~***~

Shadows.

They flickered and danced along the basement walls; strange, ghostly figures erupting each time Emmett lit another candle.

Zari and Jessa had rounded up more towels and blankets and hovered over Livvie and her little girl. Sopping, fuchsia blanket discarded and thumb in her mouth, the child stared somberly at the motley crew gathered in the basement corner. "What's her name?" Zari felt a visceral pull in her gut toward the baby, a wanting so powerful it brought a tear to her eye. She shut her eyes hard, and bit her lip. "She's adorable."

"Iris. Her name is Iris. She's fourteen months old." With thick brown curls, bright violet eyes and round, flushed pink cheeks, Iris was as vibrant as her mother was faded. Dimpled fists opened and shut in Zari's direction. "I can't thank you enough for letting us come in. I was so scared she would get hurt out there."

"No worries. I'm just glad we heard you knocking over the thunder. Are you warm enough?"

"I am. Thanks." Livvie's smile was weak, but seemed genuine. The glow of the candlelight accentuated the purple smudges beneath her eyes, the color a glaring contrast to her otherwise pale features. A crude, heart-shaped scar interrupted the porcelain skin of her left cheek.

"Babe." Emmett's voice was low, urgent. Zari stood, smiling reassuringly at Jess and Livvie and walked in a deliberately slow manner to her husband. He was staring at his smartphone, his face puckered as though he had an entire lemon sitting on his tongue. His opposite hand was doing that thing —that odd little habit he had of touching the tips of his fingers to his thumb, one at a time and back again. He did it when he was nervous or felt out of control. Zari had noticed the quirk years ago and found it strangely endearing. The corner of her mouth twitched in a half-smile. "A tornado touched down about five miles from here, and it's headed this way. Took the roof off a hardware store." Anxiety was evident in the crack of his voice, the fiddling with his wireframes, the repetitive bobble of his Adam's apple.

Her smirk disappeared. Twirling the tie-strings of her pajama bottoms with her finger, Zari opened her mouth to whisper, but Miss Maylie's screams drowned out any thoughts she might have had. "A tornado! It's comin'!" Her hand lay over her chest as if protecting her heart from the raging storm. Mr. Grady draped his arm around her shoulders, murmuring words of comfort in a useless attempt to quiet his hysterical wife. "I hear it! I hear it!"

she sobbed, "Sounds like a train!" Once uttered, the entire crowd heard the horrific sound, a ferocious engine barreling closer and closer. Iris began to cry, a howling siren of a scream quickly mimicked in canine baritone by Rocko. Livvie's tears were instantaneous, but silently dripped down her face, a waterfall of exhausted emotion. Jessa, ever the mothering sort in a crisis, was hushing and patting and comforting, smiling against the liquid in her own eyes even as the shaking of her hands was apparent. Zari wrapped her arms around Emmett, her head leaning against the strength of his shoulder.

"I don't know what to do, Zari. I feel like Noah, watching the Ark sink. I'm responsible for keeping all these people safe." He rubbed his forehead, then the bridge of his nose.

"Let's not be quite so dramatic, Emmett. This isn't the Ark. We've only got one dog here," she said dryly.

One corner of his mouth raised in a smirk at her comment. "You know what I mean. I'm running through every bit of tornado safety advice I've ever heard, but I feel frozen."

"I think we should get everyone into the utility room. No windows in there, and if we prop that old table back up, a few of them could fit under it."

Spurred into action, Emmett moved toward the center of the group and began giving directions. His deep voice commanded attention, and each face turned to him, listening. He deliberately kept his voice low and controlled as he explained the plan. Obedient, the group rose and crowded into the small room that housed their washer and dryer, kicking aside the fallen laundry soap jugs. "Mr. Grady, can you help me? I need that wood glue up there on that shelf," Emmett asked as he slid his lanky frame beneath the broken table, positioning the busted table leg back where it belonged. The two men worked together quickly, stabilizing the makeshift shelter. Jessa held a flashlight and a candle in their direction, the dim flicker of light a small help to their operation. Zari stood behind them, holding Iris and bouncing her softly up and down. The baby's frantic shrieks had died down to the persistent, plaintive hum of a tired infant. Livvie worked swiftly and quietly, folding up the blankets and carrying the stack to the little room, spreading the thickest one on the floor under the table.

"Livvie, you go on and get down there, and I'll hand you the baby." Zari's voice was insistent. "You, too, Miss Maylie. Emmett, help her down, please." Without a word, they collectively agreed to ensure the safety of the most vulnerable, first. The elderly woman grunted, her bones crackling as she crawled under the table. "Mr. Grady, can you fit down there with her? Let's see if you can. Go on."

Mr. Grady's mouth hung open, horrified at the notion of putting his safety before that of a woman. "Baby Girl," his tone was one of utter disgust, "I would *never*! You get down there. You just a young thing."

Fire lit her eyes, and her chin rose up an inch. "This is *my* home, and it's my job to keep you safe! Now get down there with your wife!" Zari pointed angrily at the remaining inches of floor space beneath the wobbly-legged table.

Mr. Grady folded his considerable arms across his chest, just as stubborn as his counterpart. "I will not. And don't you raise your voice at me, child. Ain't respectful."

Zari glared at the old man, fear igniting the ire in her words.

"Fine!" her eyes never broke his determined stare. "Jessa! *You* get down there!" Opening her mouth to protest, but thinking better of it, Jessa got down on her knees, squeezing herself into the tiny space. Mr. Grady grinned, then whistled for his dog. "Rocko! Come on in here now!" The big dog ambled in, obediently sitting next to his master with a befuddled expression on his face.

Emmett slammed the thin wooden door separating the utility room from the rest of the basement, and slid down the innermost wall of the room. Wrapping a blanket around his back and holding his arms up, he invited Zari to sit with him, and when she sat on his lap, he crossed his arms over her, covering her with the blanket in the process. Outside, the great, hammering sound of a train engine seemed to be surrounding them. Emmett reached back to rub his neck, tension knotting a clenching pain at the tip of his spine. Mr. Grady sat down hard on the chair he'd carried in, resting his face in his hands and elbows on his knees.

Zari tipped her head up to look at Emmett, who dropped a kiss on her forehead. "You've got bloody dreads, babe. Gross."

"Well. At least the bleeding stopped. The way it was gushing at first, I thought it might need stitches."

"Yeah, well I…wait…hear that?"

"What is…oh my God, Emmett. It's on us, isn't it?" The walls of the basement trembled with the frightening roar of furious nature.

"I think so. " He held her tight, squeezing her body against his, painfully aware that in this situation, the strength of his body could not protect his wife. Yet he gripped her body and pulled her closer, as if to somehow melt her body into his for safekeeping.

"It's okay, we're all right. We're all right."

Zari did not find his mantra reassuring and clenched her teeth against their chattering.

Jessa drew her knees up to her chest and buried her face in them, her short, shallow breaths giving away the hyperventilation she was attempting to hide. Livvie stood on her knees and turned her body so the baby was nearest the corner, and curled herself around the sleeping Iris.

"Heaven help us!" Miss Maylie whispered in the darkness, crossing herself repeatedly. "Father God, Baby Jesus. Help us, help us. James!" Mr. Grady rose from his seat and knelt before her, reaching his hand toward hers and clasping it firmly. "We'll be fine, Maylie. We'll be fine. Don't be scared, now."

Any further words were swept away in the rushing echo of terror invading the basement.

Chapter Three

In the Thick.

"Little Red Riding Hood
I don't think little big girls should
Go walking in these spooky old woods
Alone."
-Ronald Blackwell, *Hey There Little Red Riding Hood*

    The eerie stillness of the trees belied the havoc so recently wreaked by the devastating storm. Emmett and Mr. Grady—each wielding flashlights—neared the sliding glass doors at the back of the farmhouse, cautiously. Emmett undid the locks and slid the door open, stepping out onto the porch.
    He was unprepared for the abrupt tumble he was met with. "What the h – ...?" His foot stepped out on nothing but air and he lurched into the black night, arms flailing. *THUD!* Emmett's back hit the ground hard, knocking the wind out of him. He slapped a muddy hand over his forehead, rubbing his temples. "Mother f—..." Emmett remembered the older man standing just inside the doorway, "...f-fudge."

    "How's that now? You all right, boy?" James Grady squinted out into the darkness.

    "Yeah, I just—apparently we no longer have a back porch." Struggling to his feet, he brushed at the filthy sludge sinking through his khakis, attempting to curb his aggravation.

    "Ain't that a shame, though? After all the work you kids just got done on it." James Grady pursed his lips and made a slight sucking sound.

"What work?" He blinked, his face honestly blank.

"You know. Zari was over my place the other day, telling me how hard you'd all been working out here. "

"I…" Emmett thought for a moment, all at once remembering their passionate night on the porch beneath the stars. "Oooohh, yeah. Right. All that work we've been doing. Such a shame!" He blushed a fiery red in the darkness, thankful for the cover of night. Raising his brows, Emmett grinned. He held up a rough chunk of ice as big around as an orange. "Look at the size of this hail, though. You ever seen anything like this? Isn't it crazy? Bet this left some dents in my truck. Man."

The women were clustered together around the kitchen table, the five large candles in the center of it barely lighting the room. Zari had boiled water on the gas stove, and fixed them each a cup of chamomile tea. Miss Maylie sat with shoulders hunched, sadly shaking her head at the injustice Mother Nature had dealt. The older woman had dark brown freckles sprinkled across her wide, caramel colored face and tightly curled hair that once had been a brassy blond but was now interspersed with white. Jessa had found a container of chocolate chip cookies and was devouring them at breakneck speed. Livvie was bouncing a fussy Iris with a weariness that seemed far too old for her age. "I think she's hungry," she said.

Zari opened the fridge and peered in. "Um, I've got rice milk…"

"Rice huh?" Livvie's face twisted in confusion.

"Milk. I'm sorry, I'm out of the regular variety. Emmett's the only one who drinks it. But rice milk would work, wouldn't it?"

"Oh, um, I...I breastfeed. It won't bother you guys, will it?" The hungry baby was grabbing at Livvie's shirt with her tiny, dimpled fists. With surprising confidence, Livvie lifted one side of her shirt and arranged Iris for a feeding with as much modesty as she could muster. Miss Maylie and Jessa politely averted their eyes, but Zari stood transfixed. *I want this. With all my heart and all my soul, this is what I want in my life. I want to carry Emmett's child inside me, and then nourish it with my own body, watching our baby grow and giggle and crawl and walk. It isn't fair that my genetics have stolen this from me. It isn't fair!* Swallowing against the dry lump growing in her throat, Zari turned away. The very sight of the nursing child was so perfectly precious, it caused a deep, visceral pain within her; the ache of loss for something she'd never had.

"You should eat, Livvie. Let me see what I can find for you." Zari leaned into the refrigerator, squinting in the wavering candlelight. "Yogurt? Apple?"

"Anything is fine. Thanks." Zari tossed an apple through the air and Livvie caught it with her free hand, smiling. "I'm so glad you guys opened the door for me. And I'm glad you aren't, like, serial killers or whatever."

Jessa and Zari laughed. Even the corners of Miss Maylie's mouth turned up a bit.

"Zari! Come here for a second." Emmett's voice cut through their laughter, and Zari paused. He sounded awfully serious. "Coming!" She picked a candle up off the table and gingerly made her way through the living room. "Emm...?"

"Over here." He stood near the sliding glass doors still, conscious of the fresh mud that now covered him, dripping occasionally from his clothes in a soft *plop* on the floor. As Zari approached, he reached a dirty hand out, squeezing her shoulder gently.

"What's going on? Is everything okay?" He looked so solemn, her heart caught for a second.

"I need to tell you something, babe." He took a deep breath and reached out to hold her hands. His thumbs pressed into her palms. "The storm ripped off the back porch. I mean, it's entirely gone."

Her eyes widened. "The whole porch?" Surely, he couldn't mean that.

"The whole porch." He sounded grim.

"Wow."

"Yeah. I know. But at least no one here was hurt. We can rebuild it." Emmett didn't sound excited at this possibility.

"Yeah. I just hope the storms are over. This entire day has been crazy."

"I think our guests may as well stay the night, just in case. Better safe than sorry, right? Maybe tomorrow I can take a look at Livvie's car, see if we can get it running for her." Now and again, when he could force and keep his attention span on one topic for a length of time, he found he had a knack for mechanics.

"Okay." Zari sounded somewhat doubtful. "I'll go let them know."

The closer Zari came to the kitchen, the louder the clatter emanating from the room became. Tipping her candle toward the kitchen, Zari saw Miss Maylie hustling about the table, setting out fixings for sandwiches. Seeing Zari, she said, "Our men will need to eat. I do, too. Got the sugar, you know." Oh, right. Zari had forgotten Miss Maylie was diabetic. She should have eaten long before now. "You get on up now, get some plates for us." Jessa was on her feet with a "Yes, ma'am" immediately.

"So, guys, listen. Emmett and I were talking, and we think you guys should all just stay here for the rest of the night. Just in case another round of storms roll in. We've got plenty of blankets, pillows, everything. And Livvie, Emmett said he'll take a look at your car in the morning, okay?"

Murmurs of assent echoed through the kitchen. Zari set about locating more quilts and setting up makeshift beds on the living room floor. "Miss Maylie, you get the couch, ma'am. No arguments."

The familiar action of laying out bedding was comforting to Zari. Snapping the wrinkles from the sheets, folding heavy quilts in half and straightening the pillows until they were just right eased the tension from her shoulders and helped to slow her racing thoughts. The collective adrenaline rush that had been present during the tornado was seeping out of each of them and exhausted, the group shuffled to their respective sleeping spots. Livvie turned down a thick patchwork quilt at the end of the row and seemed to melt into the blanket, curling her small frame around her already sleeping daughter. Jessa slid into the next blanket, followed by Mr. Grady. The cracking of his joints was audible as he moved slowly from a standing position to his knees, and finally managed to crawl into a flat position on the floor. As he situated his blanket he reached up to hold his wife's hand. Miss Maylie locked her hand into his and within minutes the only sound in the living room was that of her soft snoring. Rocko curled up at his master's feet, gratefully resting his head against the floor and closing his eyes.

Emmett reached for Zari's hand as they ascended the stairs, considering. Their life was happy, to be sure, but quiet and rather solitary. Having a houseful of guests was a new experience, but something about having their home crowded and noisy simply felt right. Strange, but right. He squeezed Zari's hand, enjoying the feel of her soft, slender fingers in his. They'd made it through the storm, and while there was damage to be tended to in the morning, they'd survived. He'd done his job and kept his family safe.

At that moment, he felt absolutely invincible.

~***~

Something was wrong.

Zari knew it, even as she fought against the nightmare that had engulfed her. Thrashing about in her mind as well as in the bed, she pushed herself to awaken. She was trapped in that gauzy middle ground between hard sleep and clarity.

And she was suffocating.

The snake was everywhere: over her, inside of her, shoving itself into her eyes, her mouth, her belly. A serpent bigger than she was, it filled most of the room. Couldn't Emmett see it? Didn't he hear the hissing, the horrible echoing of it that was hammering her ears? The air was heavy, tangible, too thick to breathe in and she struggled for air, arching her back in a desperate attempt to suck in oxygen. The gigantic serpent slid over her, releasing a sickening slurping sound with each movement. Zari could feel the slime dripping off of her. She shuddered, squeezing her eyes shut. It was melting into her, sealing its revolting body to hers with a scalding heat that made her cry out in agony. "No!" she cried out. "No, no, no!" The snake laughed, a hideous, wheezing sound that left goose bumps on her skin.

"Zari! You are one of us! You are one *with* us!"

"No!"

"We are Slither! We are bound together!"

"I won't! I won't do this!"

Horrendous cackling filled the room, permeating the air, sticking to her skin like a layer of filth.

Zari's eyes snapped open and watched in terror as the face of the serpent dissolved into the face of the little girl, Kayde, smiling prettily. The face stretched and changed again, this time to a face once dear to Zari, one she hadn't seen in many years. Chocolate brown hair buzzed short enough to show skin peeking through it. Short enough that it felt soft as the first sweet locks of an infant. Narrow violet eyes set in deep sockets with puffy dark pockets of flesh sitting immediately below them. A wide red mouth with deep, puckered lines about the lips. Impossibly straight, white teeth. Square chin. Nan's features were older and seemed to have softened in some ways and in others looked harsh and wrinkled.

"N—Nan?" It couldn't be possible. Could it?

"Child. You've been gone so long. You've got to come home now. It's time for you to accept your gift," Nan said, warm and inviting.

"I don't want it. I won't be like you, like Mama. I want to be normal," Zari said, insistent.

"Normal? What, like this poor excuse of a man you've chosen to bed?"

"Leave Emmett out of this. I love him. I'm happy. He doesn't know about...this, and he isn't going to. Isn't there any way I can get out of it?" Her voice was desperate, pleading.

"Get out of it? Renounce your bloodline? How do you propose to do that?" A harsh, barking laugh escaped Nan's lips.

"I don't know! Just...get it out of me!" Zari cried.

Suddenly, Nan was human again. Sitting atop Zari's chest, she set about her grim task—wrapping a transparent film about Zari's head. Horrified, Zari attempted to reach up to stop her, only to find her arms were cuffed to the bed. Digging the back of her head into the pillow, Zari screamed.

Nan wrapped the film tightly around Zari's face, pulling hard as she stretched the film to wrap around her head one more time. Nan grinned broadly as she worked.

Emmett, Emmett, Emmett! Help me!

She was suffocating. There was no air, no air...

~***~

Zari wasn't breathing. Her eyes and mouth were wide open; face ashen, lips cyanotic. The final shudder of breath had left her, and she was cold and deathly still. The temperature of her skin against his or the stillness or the lack of sound from her breathing woke Emmett with a start. His brain knocked at his consciousness, telling him something was wrong and he sat up, blinking and looking around the room. The window was shut, the door was shut, nobody in the room. He listened for the sound of sirens or trains or lightning cracking trees in half and heard none. What was it then? Emmett reached for Zari's arm, shaking it lightly. "Babe. Did you hear anything?" When Zari didn't respond, he looked down and was horrified by what he saw. "Zari!" The strangled scream was a heartbreaking sound. "No! *No!*" The simple word was drawn out into a siren wail, rising and falling and rising again. He was on top of her in an instant, the sinewy muscle of his thighs tightening against her, the round, protruding bones of his ankles digging into the flesh of her thighs. He placed his palms strategically above her sternum, *push pause push pause push pause* .

"Emmett? Is everything okay?" Jessa had been startled awake by his shouting and peered into the room, the door just a couple inches ajar. "Oh my God, Emmett! What happened? Is she breathing?"

"Jessa! Call," *push pause push pause*, "…call 911! Hurry!"

Jessa's only response was to turn and run back down the stairs and hope to high heaven her cell phone had some battery juice remaining. The power in the house was still out.

Dawn was just breaking and the pink and orange sky allowed just a bare bit of light into the lower level of the farmhouse. Through the windows, storm damage was evident as trees lay across the road and in the driveway and the yard. Chunks of the beautiful back porch were scattered in the front yard, the steps separated but still recognizable. Black clouds sat fat and angry above the sunrise, an omen of the misery it was preparing to bring to a town already bleak with destruction.

Out of breath, Jessa blew into the living room, rummaging through her purse for her phone. "Please, please, please," she whispered. Her hand clutched at the device and her heart sank as she realized there was no light emanating from the screen. "*Shit*," she said aloud. "Livvie? Livvie!" The young mother woke with a gasp. "What's wrong? Where's Iris?" Jessa glanced around and saw the little girl had rolled around in her sleep, ending up several feet away amidst a pile of blankets. "She's over there. She's fine. I need your phone. Something's wrong with Zari. I don't think she's breathing." Yanking the phone from her pocket, she tossed it to Jessa and quickly jumped to a standing position. "You call. I know CPR. I'll go help Emmett. Which one is their room?"

"Top of the stairs, first on the right."

Livvie ran, repeating the steps for CPR aloud in a whisper. Slamming the bedroom door open with the heel of her hand she burst into the bedroom and felt instant empathy for Emmett, who had broken out in a sweat with rivers of heat running down his face and bare chest. His own breath was coming in short little spurts. Emmett's curls were wild, standing out in every direction. Livvie paused for just a second in the dim light, taking in the sight of the straight and narrow, sort of geeky man of the house with his shirt off and tattoos lacing his back and upper arms. She blinked. Livvie liked tattoos and finding out he had these hidden beneath his buttoned-up exterior lit a fire low in her belly. She shook her head. The bad, tatted up guys she liked always turned out causing her nothing but heartache. Besides, this particular guy was clearly taken. And his wife wasn't breathing. She despised herself all over again. So much was wrong with her, obviously. Wanting guys she shouldn't have was only one on a never ending list of Livvie's "Reasons I Hate Myself. "Emmett. *Emmett.* Let me take over. Take a break. I know how to do it. And Jessa's calling 911 right now." Still compressing Zari's chest, Emmett turned his head toward Livvie. His eyes met hers and her heart cracked a bit at the bleak despair that covered his face. His chin trembled and the little hollow at the base of his neck sucked in hard with each compression. "Have you given any breaths?" Emmett shook his head. No. "Okay then. Stop for a minute." Reluctantly, Emmett dropped his hands to his sides and sat back, straddling his pale, still wife. His chest heaved and he gulped air, wiping the sweat from around his eyes with the back of his hands. Livvie climbed onto the opposite side of their bed, pushing aside quilts of varying colors as she did so. Placing her right hand beneath the neck and tipping Zari's head back, she immediately pinched Zari's nose shut and pressed her mouth to the silent blue lips of the dreadlocked girl lying so still in the bed.

"I just…I just woke up and she was like this. I looked at her and she was so quiet and her…God her face was like that with her eyes open and blue lips. Oh my God. Is this real? Is it real? Is my wife dead? Oh. Oh." Emmett held his arms across his stomach and bent over, vomit rushing unbidden from the depths of him, filling his throat and nose and cheeks at once, bursting forth on the floor with unbelievable force. Grabbing the corner of a quilt, he wiped at his mouth. Turning back, he saw Livvie performing the same actions he'd just been doing himself. Emmett looked at his hands, turning them before his face in the dim light. Had he really just been doing CPR on his Zari? Had his hands just been forcing air into his dead wife's lungs?

Jessa rounded the corner and ran into the room, phone in hand. "Emmett. Listen." She stopped and looked at her precious friend's husband. He looked terrible. Beautiful, but terrible. Livvie, tiny as she was, was breathing air into Zari's lungs and pushing on her chest in a valiant attempt to keep her alive. Her light hair was darkened with damp sweat, sticking to her forehead and cheeks. Zari looked—well. Zari looked dead. Jessa was filled with overwhelming sadness and panic at once, and wished she could release the feeling boiling inside her by screaming or crying but was choked by the numbness that spread throughout her insides. "They're coming, okay? But it's going to take a while. They're having trouble maneuvering around the trees and vehicles that are blocking the roads. But they'll find a way. They said they'll come." He looked so pitiful, his eyes scanning the room in search of anything that might help the unreal situation they'd found themselves in.

"I don't know what to do. Jessa, what do I do?" He fluttered his hands helplessly in the air in front of him. His voice cracked. "How did this happen? I don't…I don't understand, Jess. She was fine. Everything was fine."

Jessa's soul ached for Emmett. The feelings she held for the husband of her best friend were just that – feelings. Jessa was attracted—had always been attracted to him. But she would never have acted on those emotions —at least, she didn't think she would. She loved Zari, and the way she felt for Emmett was more than friendship. Beyond his obvious physical attributes, Emmett was just one of those men, those last few honorable guys that seemed to be the embodiment of every romantic notion she'd hoped for since adolescence. Of any couple she'd known, Zari and Emmett's relationship had always been an example of what a true marriage should be. Each of them loved the other devotedly and that was obvious. Wrecking that fairytale wasn't something Jessa wanted to live with, so she determined to live parallel to the love story instead. It hadn't been easy; now and again, a shot of jealousy overwhelmed her. Jessa shook her head to clear it. Now was not the time to dwell on Emmett; Zari needed her. She could only imagine how horrifying this had to be for the poor guy. And she knew that of the crew currently assembled at the house, she was the only one Emmett really knew well. She had to be the one to try and comfort him. Slowly, she forced her legs to propel toward the bed. It was difficult, because the freezing numbness had spread to her legs. Jessa took the final step toward the bed, wrapping her arms around Emmett's shoulders and drawing him in to her abdomen. She slipped her hand into his hair and bent down to whisper in his ear. Something felt strange on the sole of her foot. "We have to believe she'll be okay, Em. We've got to have faith she can make it through this. And I want you to know, no matter how this turns out, I'm here for you. I'll always be here for you, Emmett. I'm going to help you through it. But right now we have to just believe in Zari, believe she'll be okay. Do you…do you want me to pray with you?" Emmett gulped and nodded his head against her stomach. Her foot felt sticky. Sticky and wet. Jessa thought back, remembering her childhood days at the church her parents belonged to. The swell of the organ music, the dark blue upholstered pews. Hands held and familiar hymns sung. Stained glass windows. She closed her eyes. "Dear God. Please be with Zari. Please make her start breathing again. And please find a way for help to get here soon. Um. Amen." It'd been so long since she'd prayed to God, and Jessa's lips were rusty at the practice of it. Her eyes opened and she looked down at Emmett who was still leaning against her. Her eyes traveled further, down to the floor. She was standing in a pool of chunky green vomit. Jessa gagged and swallowed hard.

Livvie was drenched in sweat. It dripped down her face and pooled across the chest of her shirt, leaving a dark, wet stain. "Em. Emmett." Her voice was dry, her breaths coming fast. "I need you to take over. I'll do the breaths. You do the compressions." Emmett lumbered in slow motion as he stood and turned, taking Livvie's place. He heard an incredibly loud sound roaring at them and winced. "Is it storming? Is that another tornado?" The stress had him nearly collapsing as he tried to force his mind to think of what to do if they had to get Zari to the basement. He came up blank.

    Jessa was at the window, searching. The sky was darkening, but not terribly ominous. She cracked the window: no sirens, no train sound like they'd heard earlier. But the deafening sound was certainly getting closer. Then she saw it: "Emmett! They're here! The helicopter is here for Zari!" She flew from the room and down the stairs, out the front door. Waving her arms above her head she shouted, "Here! Down here! Help!" and the helicopter came down, right down on the ground between shards of wood and downed tree branches. A man and a woman jumped from the helicopter and grabbed bags, equipment and a stretcher, tucked their treasures under their arms. They looked to Jessa for direction. "This way!" She shouted over the blaring sound coming from the craft, waving with her arms to indicate they should follow her into the house. The helicopter pilot remained in his craft and waited for his crew and patient to return. They ran in a line, Jessa at the head. She was still screaming as she relayed the story. "She was fine last night; in fact we were up until early morning due to the storm. Her husband woke up just a short while ago and she wasn't breathing. He started compressions and another woman who is here started doing full CPR. First door on the right." The medics rushed into the room and to the bed, murmuring to one another as they set about their task. The female was checking for Zari's pulse and listening for breaths. She was pulling equipment from her bags, arranging the stretcher to lie directly next to Zari's unconscious body.

    Numb and still feeling as if they were trapped in some surreal group dream, the three stepped mechanically down the stairs. Their solemn descent was startled by the female medic shouting, "Bag her! *Now!*" Livvie jolted and Emmett stumbled, grabbing out for —but missing—the stair railing as his long legs folded and he floated unceremoniously above the last three steps and landed hard on his back on the floor. Knocked utterly empty of wind, Emmett arched his body against the pain ricocheting through his frame. After the initial gasp that echoed throughout the room, several short, forced blasts of air shot from his mouth. Emmett's hands moved awkwardly, jumping back and forth in the air around his body and finally resting on his face, covering his eyes. Jessa and Livvie had managed to catch hold of each other and lean against the wall, effectively stopping one another from falling and they watched him, frozen with pity. With one jerky motion, Emmett drew his knees up to his chest and rolled onto his right side, the harsh breaths that had been knocked loose erupting into rasping, gut-wrenching sobs. The bent wire frame of the left side of his glasses could be seen poking out from above his hand. Sleep-wrinkled khakis were all that he wore and his considerable shoulders shook with the effort of his weeping. Sounds emanating from the bedroom above them became louder with each passing second: the crumbling of plastic discard from hurriedly unwrapped medical equipment, the male medic's voice counting out compressions, their muted voices murmuring to one another. The voices rose, "One, two, *three* !" and there were heavy footsteps walking in practiced unison out of the bedroom and down the hall. Mr. Grady stepped around the crumpled body of his young friend and knelt down placing his worn, brown hands on Emmett's shoulders, turning and lifting his dead weight. "Emmett. Son. Come on. Come with me, now." Emmett struggled to his feet, still weeping, his shuddering chest sucking great gulps of air. He leaned down at least six inches to wrap his arms around the older man, soaking the neck and shoulder fabric of James' shirt with his tears. "What will I do? What will I do?" he mumbled. James Grady had seen plenty of pain in his lifetime, and his heart wept for this man, his friend, who'd fought so hard for the life he'd built and was watching it dissipate before his eyes. Clearing his throat, James clapped Emmett hard on the back the way men do when words fail, and whispered simple, broken phrases like "son" and "all right" and "me too, me too." The medics padded deftly down the stairs behind them, Zari's unresponsive body strapped to their board, her shockingly white face looking alien with the bag that was keeping her breathing standing up and to the side of her slack mouth. A dribble of dried blood was smeared on her chin, and her dreads spilled haphazardly off the stretcher. The male medic walked backward at the head of the board, his right hand white-knuckled in the hand hold of it, his left hand tirelessly working the bag for Zari's breaths. The female medic's hands strained to hold the corners of the stretcher as they made their way to the door. Zari's bare feet poked out from beneath the grey wool blanket she'd been wrapped in. Livvie scrambled to hold the door open for them as they shouted directions over the near deafening hum of the helicopter. "Not enough room in the craft for more people! ETA fifteen minutes if you can find a way to Mercy Park Hospital! We heard there was a clean-up initiated on I-90 if you can make it that way!"

    Zari was loaded into the helicopter, and just as she grabbed hold of the handle to hoist herself into the craft, the female medic looked back at the house, at the group of people and the big dog gathered on the porch. Her eyes zeroed in on the shirtless, lanky brown-haired man with his shoulders hunched and hands covering his mouth. The husband. Poor guy. She hoped his support system was solid, because it wasn't looking good for his wife. She slapped the side of the helicopter twice and it rose, slowly at first but gaining speed as it turned and headed toward the center of town.

    Emmett watched it go, watched it becoming smaller and smaller until the helicopter carrying Zari was just a dot in the distance, a dark spot in the skyscape indistinguishable from the host of ominous, blackening clouds rolling at them.

Another storm was coming. Emmett leaned over, sucking breath after breath with his hands on his knees. The air was stifling. Abruptly, he stood and stalked back into the house, standing tall with purpose. Emmett hustled about the room, filling his pants pockets with his cell phone and charger, wallet—he'd found it under the end table—and taking off his glasses to right the bent side of the frame. Sockless, he jammed his feet into worn brown work boots and walked over to the windows, opening the blinds. The shock of light caused each of them to squint against it. "Jessa, could you run upstairs and grab me a shirt?" His voice was deep and heavy with emotion. Without a spoken reply, she hurried up the stairs. Miss Maylie had carried a fussing Iris over to Livvie, who plopped down on the couch and too exhausted to consider modesty, lifted the side of her shirt to nurse. Arms emptied, Maylie paced and rubbed her upper arms as if to ward off a chill. "Let me fix you something to eat, boy." Emmett waved her off even as she headed to the kitchen, the sounds of plates hitting the table and the opening and shutting of the refrigerator door filling the overly quiet farmhouse. Mr. Grady stepped toward him. "Son, look I know you need to go to her. What're you thinking?" From what could be seen, the roads looked treacherous, but James knew there would be no stopping Emmett. If it had been his own Maylie, wouldn't he have moved heaven and earth to get to her? Of course.

"I'm just going to head out in my truck. Get as far as I can. Walk or hitch if I have to stop. I've, I've…I've gotta…." Momentarily, Emmett's resolve abandoned him and his chin quivered. He ran his hand through his curls and swallowed against the fear. "I'm going to do whatever I can. I just need to go. "

Jessa appeared in the living room, a rumpled faded green button-down in her hands. Holding it up, she walked toward Emmett, intending to lay the shirt over his bare shoulders. A step away from him, Jessa caught sight for the first time of his back in the light, and gasped at the grotesque scars decorating his flesh. Above the lash marks that ran at least five inches deep on the right side of his lower back was a Jim Morrison quote: "You feel your strength in the experience of pain" in green ink next to an image of an anchor. The abused skin was rippled in areas giving it an unnaturally thick, bubbled effect highlighted by various shades of pinkish-purple intermingled with a contrast of stark white, where pigmentation had been sacrificed in the fight to heal. The perfectly rounded cigarette burns that ran parallel to Emmett's spine had pocked and pitted over the years, leaving deep reddish scars that would never lighten. The uncomfortable silence was telling, and Emmett cleared his throat.

"Found something interesting to look at, huh?" he said bitterly, aggravated to have been caught unaware with his past on display like some circus freak. James and Livvie quickly planted their eyes on the floor.

Jessa startled and attempted to backtrack, "Emmett, I'm so sorry. I didn't know you were a victim of…"

Squaring his shoulders, Emmett spun angrily. "I'm not a *victim* of anything." He spat the words with a forcefulness none of them had ever heard from the generally mild-mannered man and yanked the shirt from her hands, slipping it easily over his long arms and buttoning it up as he stared out the window at the destruction and desolation. "It was a long time ago," he said through his teeth. "What matters is now."

'What matters is now.' Those were the words that arched

above the Celtic victory symbol on his left shoulder blade.

Emmett turned down the collar of his shirt and grabbed his truck keys. "If you'll excuse me, I'm going to see my wife."

His demeanor had changed so abruptly, so thoroughly, in the space of just a few moments that he seemed almost another man entirely. Guarded arrogance immediately consumed him. The difference in Emmett's voice, gait, even the unusually firm set of his jaw appeared as oddly natural to him as if he'd simply slipped inside the skin of someone else and sunk into a new identity. They watched through the window as Emmett slammed his truck door and started the engine, backing out into his own yard and tearing out over the small downed limbs on the dirt road. Packed earth flung from behind his furiously spinning tires, creating a dirty brown rage falling through the air behind him.

Emmett made it a good ten miles into town simply by veering off the road and driving through yards when necessary. Several times, he plowed his truck right up near porches and once through the backyard of an angry elderly woman who stood in her driveway wearing an orange housecoat and shaking her fist in the air at him. He didn't care. What could they do to him? The police hadn't even been able to drive through to help with Zari so he doubted they'd come after him for his less than typical driving route. Besides, eventually he did come to a stop in the road. A toppled thick-trunked, centuries-old tree completely covered the path to anywhere, the gigantic branches and roots seemingly never-ending in their reach in any direction. So singularly focused was Emmett that he simply locked up his truck and struck out on foot. He could hear the thunder crashing at least a couple of miles behind him, and slowly broke into a jog, then a run. He'd excelled at cross-country in high school and he mentally felt his muscles, reminding himself how to pace his stride and breaths. Another five miles to the hospital. He could beat the storm, he was sure. He tried to remain focused, mapping out the fastest path he could take to make it to Zari. Passing houses with trees now residing in the attics, small cars turned on their sides and the occasional homeowner taking inventory of his losses, his lungs were filled with fire and the spasms in his calf muscles were nearly his undoing. Sweat dampened his hair and the front and back of his shirt before the rain caught up to him, pummeling him with painful, ice-like drops. The sudden coolness of the air tasted sweet on his tongue as he gulped it in steady rhythm. Emmett had been running at least an hour when the hub of the city came into view, the hospital not much farther ahead. Traffic lights sat useless in the middle of the paved street intersections like confused drunks. An unusual silence engulfed the city. The pounding of his boots on the wet pavement reverberated a beat in his brain along with the only word he was cognizant of: Zar-ri, Zar-ri, Zar-ri, Zar-ri.

Emmett's mind would not accept the possibility that his wife would not be awake and alert when he arrived, wrapping her arms around him the way she often did and leaning her head against his shoulder.

His mind refused to acknowledge any inkling of that possibility.

His heart, however, was shredding itself to rags as he ran through the rain, claps of thunder at his heels.

Chapter Four

Waiting to Exhale.

*"Head under water and you tell me
To breathe easy for awhile
The breathing gets harder
Even I know that."*
-Sarah Bareilles, *Love Song*

    The receptionist barely registered Emmett's rough condition as she looked up through her bifocals. Since the storm had hit last night, all kinds had been past her desk. "Can I help you, sir?"
    Still attempting to catch a decent deep breath, Emmett rasped out, " My. Wife. Zari Delaney. She came in on the chopper. I need to…I need to see her." Fatigue overwhelmed him and he leaned against the desk, elbows smacking on the hard white wood and sending painful little hot vibrations from hitting the funny bone up his arms. "Please. Please take me to her. "

    Emmett was a pitiful sight, to be sure. Great purple shadows lurked beneath eyes swollen from weeping, shaggy brown hair with unruly curls standing out every which way, shirt buttoned errantly with two white buttons sticking out near the collar. Wire frame glasses bent at a slight angle, he stared intently at the secretary as he gulped oxygen, stridor evident in his breaths and the pale skin around his collarbone —and between his ribs, if she could have seen it—sank in with each wobbly attempt for air. A smidge of sadness stirred in her heart for him because he was so worthy of pity at that moment, but weren't they all? All those who came to her for help and names and room numbers and information, they were all sad. All pathetic. Years ago, she'd been softhearted but time and experience had toughened her up properly. She sighed and turned her attention back to the monitor, poising her hands above the keyboard. "You said her name is Zany?"

Emmett squeezed his eyes shut in annoyance, the last ounce of patience having left him far earlier in the day and shoved his hand forcefully through his hair. "No. Zari. Z-A-R-I. Last name D-E-L...."

Brusque, she held up a hand. "I've got it. Follow me."

He'd expected the woman to be taller, somehow. Instead, as she hopped down from her seat, Karen —that's what her nametag said, Karen—Emmett realized she was at least a foot shorter than Zari, four-foot-eleven, maybe, if one was generous. She was incredibly heavyset for such a small frame. Her purple scrub pants pooled over her child-sized tennis shoes, and she snapped her shoulders back with an almost audible motion as she pounded the large silver button that magically opened the double doors leading to a cavernous hallway. The assault of sights and sounds left Emmett blinking and wishing he could shrink back from the task at hand. Karen turned left then right, and he focused on the tiny woman as she navigated the unfamiliar maze of cold tile and off–white walls and off-off-white privacy curtains drawn around moaning patients and their softly murmuring cubicle mates. The harsh fluorescent lights reflected off the newly waxed floors in a nearly blinding glow and Emmett squinted, raising his right hand to his head and rubbing his thumb and forefinger on his temples. Looking around, he was slightly comforted that as far as they'd gotten so far, they were still surrounded by living people. Ailing, uncomfortable, sometimes shouting people, but definitely alive. They rounded another corner and Karen jolted to a halt. "Look,

Mr. —ah, Delaney. Let me get a physician out here to speak with you. Stay right here." She opened and disappeared behind a door before the words fully registered in Emmett's brain, and he leaned his head back against the cool, bland wall. Exhausted, he began to feel the effects of the day shooting through his body in what seemed a sudden and brutal attack. His arms ached and burned, and his legs began to shake as if they'd been desperately chilled. The contents of his stomach boiled and lurched and the fire in his lungs erupted from his mouth in harsh, uncontrollable sobs. Unable to hold himself together any longer, Emmett slid down the wall and dropped his head to his knees. The choking, hiccupping sounds he made as he wept shook his shoulders and medical staff at the central desk peered down the hall in mild concern. The door opened, and two sets of legs came out. Karen's, short and purple, paused for just a beat then walked briskly back from whence she came. The other pair was thicker, well-muscled and clad in perfectly fitting black dress pants that puddled just right above shiny black wingtips. Through the tiny window created from the space between his elbow and knee, Emmett left his head resting against his forearm and stared at those shoes, at the tiny dots that created the signature design.

An unfamiliar voice broke through the sounds of Emmett's distress.

"Mr. Delaney? I'm Dr. Jackson. Well, Steve. You can call me Steve. I'd like to talk to you about your wife. Mr. Delaney?"

The good physician waited a moment. Two. Finally, Steve slid down the wall next to the hunched figure, his heart recognizing a heartbreaking, familiar grief. He laid a hand on Emmett's back and started rubbing in circles, speaking calm and slow with his mouth right near Emmett's ear. "Come on buddy. I need you to focus here. Breathe in your nose, out your mouth. Easy, easy. That's it. She isn't gone, Mr. Delaney, your wife is still with us and I need to speak with you so we can figure out what's going on with her. "

Wiping his reddened nose on his sleeve, Emmett inched his head up and turned to meet the eyes of doctor. Emmett blew slow, deliberate breaths through pursed lips as he fought to get control of himself.

Dr. Jackson stuck his hand out toward him. "Mr. Delaney, I'm your wife's doctor. Dr. Jackson. You can call me Steve. I'd like to discuss Zari's condition with you. Do you think you can stand up?" He held his hand out toward Emmett and Emmett took it, allowing the older man to help draw him into a standing position. "I want you to listen to me, now. We're going into this room, and you're going to see Zari looking pretty rough. She looks bad, Mr. Delaney. We had to intubate, so there is a tube sticking out of her mouth. She's on oxygen. There are several machines she is hooked up to, and those machines are helping keep her alive. But that's what you need to remember: She *is* alive. I'm told that's in great part because you started CPR immediately. You're going to have to keep yourself calm, and I want you to stay strong, and listen to what I say, all right?" Steve wasn't positive this man was going to be able to keep it together, and he kept a hand balanced across Emmett's back just in case he went down – which by the quaking clearly felt through the thin fabric of his shirt was a good possibility.

"Babe? Zari? Are you..." Emmett turned to Dr. Jackson. "Can she hear me?"

The doctor looked directly into Emmett's eyes as he spoke. "Mr. Delaney. Your wife is in a coma. Right now these machines are helping her breathe. We don't know for sure what she can hear, but we also don't know for sure she can't. Go ahead. Talk to her. Then you and I will talk some more."

Emmett stood, confliction between fear and desperation halting his steps. "Hi babe." He cleared his throat and took a shaky step forward. "I didn't…ah…" his voice wobbled and caught, sounding a bit strangled, "I didn't want to send you in the helicopter by yourself, you know? They wouldn't let me go." Finally, he was at her bedside, and pulled a cushioned blue seat up toward the head of her bed. "Zar, sweetheart, I'm so sorry this is happening. I don't understand how you got so sick like this so fast, but we'll do everything we can to take care of you. I won't leave, I won't go back home until I know I can take you with me. I just…I love you so much, babe. You know how much I love you. I need you…" here his voice broke with agony, "…I need you with me. You promised me forever, and I'm holding you to it. You have to come back, Zari, you have to come back to me." Emmett was crying again, great drops of grief rolling down his face, chin wobbling. "I can't do this without you." He looked back up at Steve for guidance. "Can I, um, am I allowed to touch her?"

"You may hold her hand, the one nearest you, without the IV in it. Just not too much stimulation, though. We're trying to keep her blood pressure steady."

Gingerly, Emmett picked up her limp hand between his two and kissed it, pressing his cheek against it. He closed his eyes, seeing her desire, her beautiful body against his in their bed was it, could that have been just a day ago? Would they ever be together that way again? An invisible kick to his gut stole his breath again, and Emmett involuntarily began to hyperventilate. Dr. Jackson came up behind him, squeezing Emmett's shoulders.

"Mr. Delaney, I know this is hard on you. Remember how you were breathing slowly, out there in the hall? I need you to go back to doing that. Keep hyperventilating, and you're going to end up passing out. Your wife needs you to be strong right now."

Emmett stood, wiping at his eyes with the edges of his shirt and readjusting his glasses. "Yeah, yeah. I know it. I just need a minute. I'm sorry, could I get some water? I ran here after my truck got stuck out there, " he waved his hand toward the window, "...in the storm, and I think I'm a little, a little dehydrated. Or something." He was feeling really bad, really warm, really cold, really ill. "I think I—I mean I think I..." He squinted at Steve, at the rapidly tunneling vision that was causing him to tilt to the side. The tiny doctor was suddenly so far away. Wind. Wind was rushing at his face, stealing his air. The room narrowed down to just a slit. "S-s-steve?" His tongue felt fat and numb in his mouth and he wondered how it could be possible for his long, gangly body to be able to float in the air so easily.

"Mr. Delaney? Mr. Delaney!" Steve saw the signs, saw the collapse beginning, but wasn't quite fast enough to catch Emmett before he went down. The bounce of Emmett's head made a horrible *thwack* against the tile and his back flopped up and down twice before settling on the floor. Dr. Jackson lurched for the red call button above Zari's bed, smacking it with the heel of his hand and spinning to kneel down next to Emmett's unconscious body. Quickly, he checked him over: Pupils, dilated. Breathing, a bit ragged but definitely moving air. Pulse, steady. Heartbeat was a bit rapid, probably from dehydration, stress. Poor lad. What a day he'd had. Imagine running all this way and in the rain, no less! Seconds later, a little blonde nurse whose name Dr. Jackson could never remember—started with an "M", he thought —was in the room, obediently following the directions he barked at her. They'd get the boy fixed up, and then he and Mr. Delaney needed to have a serious talk.

SLITHER

~***~

    Emmett tried to lie still and quiet as his mother's boyfriend held him face down on the couch. Again. The man positioned himself so he sat squarely across the nine-year-old boy's shoulder blades, rendering him helpless to fight. He laughed and took another long drag on his smoke. Emmett squirmed and attempted to cry out, but with his face held forcefully down in the pillow the sound was muffled. Three hits, five at the most on that cigarette, and the pain would come. Aaron ran his fingers up and down Emmett's small spine, rubbing each vertebra with his thumb, deciding. The light touch of his fingers left a ripple of gooseflesh in its wake. This was one of best parts: the anticipation. The placement of the pattern, the choosing of the beauty. Almost time. One more drag. His heart raced with excitement, and there it was: the perfect spot. Holding the cigarette in his long, slender fingers like a chopstick, he lowered the lit end toward the boy's supple white flesh and shivered with delight when it struck. The man tipped his nose to the air and closed his eyes, the better to enjoy the smell of singeing flesh. His breath came harder, faster. Emmett's legs bounced up and down, the pain overwhelming and the boyfriend smiled tenderly at the sight of the little body flopping like a fish out of water. He removed the cigarette to reveal his art: another perfectly round burn along the spine, just to the side of the fourth lumbar vertebrae. The masterpiece was far from finished, but perfection in art took time, he knew that. Time and practice. His plans for this particular piece were…immaculate. His mouth watered and his lips twitched almost imperceptibly as he took in his work thus far: including the new burn, there were six beautiful circles along the spine, all lined up and so straight. He had to smile at his talent. The added flavor to the piece was the still-healing flesh along the lower back where he had filleted the skin two weeks ago with quick and deliberate strikes of a whip he had purchased specifically for the purpose. Lovely. The man sighed. If only he could frame his work. A great pity, that.

    Emmett moaned, reaching up to rub his horribly aching head but the upward movement was stopped by the IV in his left hand.

Confused, he stared at his hand: the IV was held flat by some clear adhesive, and a horrendous brown and purple bruise covered the skin from wrist to knuckles. Eyes darting around his small cubicle, he took in his surroundings and immediately panic clenched his lungs. The IV, the oxygen cannula that felt so stifling across this face, the pulse oximeter on the pointer finger of his right hand, the relaxed blood pressure cuff that encircled his bicep—all of it made him feel tied down. Without thought, he leaped from the bed, yanking at the tubes and lines, ripping off the sticky adhesive and whipping the IV from his hand. Blood immediately began to leak from the fat vein. Emmett muttered low, guttural noises as he threw the cannula on the floor and stood with his hands in his hair, attempting to remember how he'd come to be here in a hospital room. He looked down at the light blue hospital gown and felt a distinct draft on his backside. Emmett pulled the inadequate fabric around his body and listened to the frantic beeping of the machines behind him. The curtain that blocked off his room space from the rest of the hospital floor snapped open, and Dr. Jackson stepped in, pulling the curtain shut behind him. He spoke to Emmett in a softly controlled voice as he confidently pressed a myriad of buttons on different equipment, stopping the irritating beeping sounds.

"I see you're awake! And you've made quite a mess here, Mr. Delaney. Had you simply pressed the call button, your nurse or I would have come in to assist you properly." Jackson stopped at the wall-mounted hand sanitizer and pressed, rubbing his hands together with cleanser then turned to a small, off-white set of drawers and retrieved a box of alcohol wipes and a roll of wrap. With thick, wavy salt and pepper hair, tender blue eyes surrounded by crow's feet and permanent purple shadows that spoke of too many nights, too many years of little or no sleep and an easy smile, Jackson looked the quintessential television physician. "Come, sit down here." He gestured to the bed. Emmett walked slowly, still exhausted, confused, and hurting. He sat at the edge of the bed and Jackson expertly lifted the blood-dirtied hand and began cleaning it with a small, square alcohol wipe. Once free of the half-dried, reddish-brown fluid, the doctor wrapped the hand up securely in a fabric wrap that stuck to itself, and sat on the bed next to Emmett. He cleared his throat but said nothing.

"Ah…thanks. Sorry for the, um, mess. I just don't like to feel held down. Freaks me out. I woke up and I felt a little panicked, couldn't figure out what exactly was going on." He held his newly wrapped hand out. "My name is Emmett, by the way. Now, what can you tell me about Zari?"

Steve Jackson shook Emmett's hand and looked directly into his eyes. He had a guess that Emmett's reaction to feeling tied down had something to do with the horrific disfigurement of his back, but said nothing. When he and Nurse M had removed his clothing to thoroughly check him over after his little incident they'd come across the scars. Empathy for the man had caused his eyes to tear for a moment. Now, though, he felt nothing but admiration for the guy. Clearly he'd overcome a great deal, and that alone was worthy of respect.

The pause in conversation allowed Emmett to piece together facts and he realized in order for him to be in this idiotic blue gown, someone must have changed his clothes. God. Humiliation twice in one day. A man could only take so much.

"So, you were the one who changed my clothes? Guessing by the look of pity of on your face, you've seen my back. Who else was gawking at me?" Emmett's tone had changed again. He sat straighter, clenched his teeth.

"Look Emmett, I've seen a lot over the years. I'm not one to judge. Clearly, you've been through something, well…terrible. I can see how you'd want to keep your scars private – that story is your own. I saw them. The nurse who came to help when you passed out and hit your head saw them. That's all.. You are seriously dehydrated. I checked your blood sugar and it was sitting at sixty. No wonder you passed out. You've got a mild concussion, but I'm not worried about that. I know today has been upsetting. But you are going to need to take better care of yourself. Mrs. Delaney is going to need your strength, Emmett. "

Emmett sat straight with his hands fisted on his knees, clenching and unclenching them. He focused on blowing out breath after breath. He felt his heart calming down a bit, the anger at having his scars seen beginning to dissipate.

"I can be a bit, um, absentminded, Steve." Emmett swallowed hard. "We were just sitting down to eat last night when the storm hit, and I don't think I got much more than a bite. People kept showing up, looking for shelter. The tornado ripped my porch off. It was crazy. Then all this went on this morning. I can't remember the last time I ate anything. I'll make it a point to remember now, though. Thanks. Now, please. Tell me about Zari. Take me to her."

Jackson reached out his right hand and placed it sturdily on Emmett's shoulder, squeezing gently. "Mrs. Delaney is in a coma. Do you understand what that means?" Emmett nodded. His mother had been in a coma before she died. Granted, she'd caused herself the coma with the overabundance of crank she'd shot up. 'Coma' was a word he was familiar with. "We still aren't sure what caused her to stop breathing in the first place, but the machines are doing that work for her at the moment. Has she had any history of heart disease or asthma?" Emmett shook his head. "What about in her family? Any major diseases in her parents or siblings?" Emmett paused.

"Ah. Zari is rather…estranged, from her family, Steve. I've never even met them and it's rare she speaks of her relatives. There is a history, um, of abuse, see. My wife prefers to focus on what's ahead rather than dwell on the past. But insofar as the information I have, her parents, maternal grandmother, and younger sister are all still living."

"I see. Are you comfortable telling me what sort of abuse was involved? It could be relevant."

"Honestly, Steve? I'm not sure. She doesn't like to talk about it, and I don't push her. I mean I…I understand." Emmett flinched. "But I can tell you, I've never…never seen any sc-scars," his voice caught on the word, "on her body. She has these terrible nightmares though. I've never seen anything like them. I mean her eyes will be open and she'll be screaming like she's on fire and she gets really pale and sometimes, sometimes I'll be watching her and thinking she's going to die, the way she looks. You know? Oh, and you know, something else that's been going on with her lately is this weird shaking."

"Shaking? Tell me about that," said Jackson, interested.

"Well it's like, like she'll be sewing – she's a quilter - or washing dishes or just sitting on the couch watching TV, right, and her hands, her arms start shaking. She tries to hide it from me, but I see it. I've tried to get her to go get it checked out, but Zari has this deep-seated fear of doctors. I mean, when she wakes up here, she's going to be really, *really* pissed off."

"Hhhmmn. I wonder…have you noticed, or has she

mentioned any vision changes during these shaking episodes? The shaking, the night terrors, both could be symptomatic of epilepsy. Do you notice any repetitive motions, such as picking at the air?"

Emmett thought back. Shook his head. "No. Not that I recall." He rolled his shoulders and dropped his head back in an effort to loosen up the tightened muscles. "God, like, my head *really* hurts."

"Yeah. You smacked it pretty good on the floor. I can get you something for that. And you're going to have to let me get another IV in your arm. You need the fluids." Emmett cringed. "I know, but you have to. However," he read the protest in Emmett's face, "once it's in, I'll take you down to visit with Zari. Deal?"

Standing and immediately feeling dizzy, Emmett reached out to grab hold of the bed. Steve jumped up and guided him back to a sitting position. "Ah, ah, ah, *sit down.* You're either in this bed or in the wheelchair I'll have brought in for you. You're a big guy, buddy, and I'm not about to haul your butt up off the floor again. You're still weak, Emmett. You've been through a lot. Give yourself a minute. Now, sit back against the bed. Let me have a looksee at the veins in your other arm. I should have the nurse doing this, but I have a feeling you'd give that little thing a run for her money. Make a fist, release, yep, just like that. Make a fist, release. Oh yeah, you've got a nice little juicy one, right *there.*" The alcohol swabs came out again, along with a little tray of packaged needles and a blue tourniquet. "All right, sit still and let's get this over with." The tourniquet barely reached around Emmett's bicep and Steve tugged to make the knot. The needle slid easily into the vein, and as Steve finished his task and capped off the IV, he spoke quietly to Emmett. "Okay, are you ready to see your wife?" Emmett nodded, swallowing against the lump in his throat. "All right then. Let me get you a wheelchair and let's go."

Emmett sat unhappily in the offered mode of transportation, the look on his face conveying how he felt: like a gorilla in a kindergartner's chair. Steve pushed him down the bland hallways, finally stopping at the door of Zari's room. "You ready? Remember, Emmett, Zari is in a coma. She will not be awake when you go in, and her condition…it isn't good, Emmett. We're hoping for the best turnout, but we don't know. Do you understand what I'm saying, Emmett?" Steve watched as his words registered in the younger man's eyes. Emmett gave a quick nod. Yes.

Zari lay perfectly still in the big hospital bed that somehow managed to make her tall frame seem tiny. Her chest pumped in a perfunctory manner, aided by the machine that stood on the side nearest the window. A quiet wheezing hum spat from the machine every few seconds, expressing an unnatural breathing rhythm that both men automatically adjusted their own to match. "She looks…she looks like she's just sleeping."

"I know." Jackson pushed him all the way to the bed and Emmett reached out, tenderly touching her face with his thumb and slowly dragging it down her jawline. It was a precious, beautiful movement, and it caused Jackson's breath to catch in his chest. He remembered…he remembered doing that same thing, dragging his own thumb down Caroline's face when…well. When the cancer had nearly finished its vile mission and her skin had been sallow and sunken and her hair was gone, but for the wisps that stubbornly held on. Even so. Even so, she'd been so beautiful. His soul had shattered, watching the disease ravage her the way it had. Saliva pooled in his cheeks at the memory, and he swallowed. Cleared his throat. Blinked rapidly. Turned away from the small but private display of affection and tried to forget the feel of

Caroline's cold skin on his thumb. Every day, every damn day of the last three years since she'd died, he'd missed her with a visceral yearning that was present from the time he woke up to the hours he tossed between sleep and wakefulness at night. But he'd been blessed, too, to have touched it, touched that sort of love so many spent their whole lives without.

Emmett and Zari had it, had that same kind of love; he could see it. Perhaps he was just projecting; Emmett reminded him so much of himself. But still. God, he hoped the girl made it.

"She's beautiful." Emmett looked up at the doctor's words, his face haggard with worry.

"Yes. She is, isn't she? Even like this. That's what her name means, you know. Zari. It means beautiful. Zari Uadjit." Emmett blew the second name out softly: *You-ahh-jee.* "Beautiful snake goddess. And yeah…she *hates* her middle name. I've never…" he stopped.

Jackson tipped his head. "Never…?"

"Never understood why she picked me. Zari , she's…so much. Everything. Beautiful. Compassionate. Creative. She's just, you know, so much *more.* I've just always felt like I've won the lottery." Emmett paused, taking a deep breath and shoving his hands through his hair again as he looked at her. Zari's dreads were a mess, tangled up all over her pillow. "Hey, Steve?"

"Yeah? "

"Her hair, having it messy like this would drive her crazy. Do you know if there's someplace around here I could get a scarf for her, so I could tie it back?"

"The gift shop, maybe. I'll ask the nurse, see if she can stop by on her break and look. That's um, her hair. Pretty unusual, isn't it? Especially of that length? Is there a particular reason for it?"

"For what? The dreads?" Emmett shrugged. "I don't know. She's always worn it this way, ever since I met her. Suits her, her personality. But it's usually tied back. She only…" his voice cracked. "She only ever lets it down and loose like this for me." Emmett swiped at another errant tear. "I just…I don't understand how we've come to this. She was fine yesterday. Everything was fine. This is killing me."

"I know." The words hung in the air, flat and solid.

"Do you?" Emmett asked, his voice unintentionally sharp.

"Yes. I do." Jackson's voice was raw, heavy with emotion. "I do." He held his hands out from his sides, palms up.

The two men stared at one another for a moment.

"That's why you've been so kind to me." It wasn't a question.

"Emmett, I'm going to do the best I can for you, for her. You can believe that. Now, if you promise to stay sitting down, I've got a couple patients I need to check in on, and I'll see what we can do about getting something to pull her hair back, all right? Deal?" Steve dipped his head down and raised his brows, earning a half-smile from Emmett. "Hopefully by the time I get back we'll have some of her test results."

The door closed softly behind Jackson as he stepped out.

Wishing he could climb up in the bed with his wife but afraid of further harming her, Emmett held her hand and tried to process the events of the day.

Regardless of how many times he deconstructed and reconstructed it, he couldn't make sense of it all. In time, exhaustion overwhelmed him and he leaned forward, resting his chin on the edge of the bed and closing his eyes.

Chapter Five

Time Tripping.

*"There's a hole in the world like a great black pit
And the vermin of the world inhabit it
And its morals aren't worth what a pig can spit."*
-Steven Sondheim, *Sweeney Todd*

Zari

Emmett.

Zari could hear his voice and feel his presence but couldn't see him. Instead, she looked up from her place on the low, hard bed at her family: Mama, Pop, Nan, and her sister, Gianna. Once again, she struggled valiantly against the straps that held her wrists down. "Let. Me. *UP!*" Zari's already throaty voice had deepened to a growl. Her long, bare legs kicked uselessly as she screamed. "I want to go home! I want to go back to Emmett!"

"Zari, child. You cannot stay with that man. He's not like us. You've got to come back home, accept your destiny. Zari, you – *we* – are Slither. You cannot disconnect yourself from the whole. You *must* learn your place within us. You must learn to feed. Slither demands it." Pop's voice – oh! It'd been so long since she'd heard it, so long since she'd seen his face. Long and craggy with high cheekbones and large round gray-green eyes – mirrors of her own – her father was still a handsome man. Six feet tall and broad shouldered with neatly trimmed blond hair and a tight smile, Pop emitted a formidable presence. As determined as she was to escape her terrifying family secret, Zari missed the days, the innocence, of the time before she'd known what they were. She'd loved him, truly. She'd loved all her family when she was small. Never had she felt so safe as she had sitting on Pop's lap, listening to one of his stories. He was so much older now; the years since she'd been gone had left trails of wear. Hardening her heart against the memories, Zari took up her fight once more.

"I don't know how many times I have to tell you this! I don't *want* to be this! Just...get me out of it somehow! I have a new life, a normal life." Zari paused to compose herself, at least a bit. "I'm married. I have a business of my own. I'm happy and I just want to be left alone. *Please.*"

"You are what you are, Zari. Your mother, Nan, none of us can change that." Pop waved his hand at the futility of even trying.

"Can't I...I want to renounce it, then! I'll do anything!" Her voice cracked with desperation.

Mama laughed, covering her mouth with her hand. Her ragged brown sweater hung past her wrists, and her dark hair had gotten stringier since last Zari had seen her. "I'm sorry, honey. You just sounded so funny. *Renounce it.*" Her mother was mocking her, raising her fingers to make quotation marks in the air. "You cannot renounce your blood, kid. You're stuck. You're part of the whole, and your man, this Emmett guy that I've never even *met*," she huffed, "you need to just be done with that nonsense." Mama threw her hands up in exasperation.

Zari let loose a shrill scream. Sweat beaded on her forehead as the sound ripped from her body. Dirt streaked her face and tears ran salty clear rivers through the grime. "Let me go, let me go, let me go!"

Nan looked at her, amused. "Feel better, now you've got that out of your system?"

Gianna stood silent in the corner, a petite version of her older sister. Her stance projected nothing so much as petulance. She flicked her forked tongue at Zari, goading her. A shiver of disgust shot through Zari at the sight of it.

Dropping back against the hard bed, Zari gulped air and tried to zero her thoughts down on some way to get out of this mess and back home. Closing her eyes, she deliberately flattened her shoulders on the bed – really, little more than an overdressed pallet – and made her voice as small as possible.

"Mama? Mama, please. I've been good. I was always a good girl for you. Always. You know that. I love him so much, just like you love Pop. Just like that. Emmett, he's a *good* man. He doesn't know anything about what we are. Please just let me have this. Let me go home to him." Her voice, her eyes were pleading.

"He doesn't know what we are? How have you managed to keep this from him?" Mama was startled; her tone was acidic.

"I just never told him."

Nan broke back into the conversation. "And the manifestations? How have you managed to keep those a secret?"

"The...the what?" More and more, it was becoming clear to her family that their secretive nature had one big drawback: their eldest daughter had left home before fully understanding who and what she was.

"The manifestations, child. Surely you've noticed. Hallucinations? Nightmares? Migraines, or perhaps you've noticed trembling, seizures even?" Nan gawked at her stupidly; her wide, red mouth like a slash of blood across her face.

Zari was silent, and her lack of communication was telling.

"Ah, so you have been affected? And exactly how long did you think you could avoid this reckoning?" Nan was obviously smug.

"I…I didn't think. I just…I just want to be normal. Isn't there some way?" Zari felt herself being drawn unwillingly back into the role of hapless child, and railed inwardly against the sensation.

"So you've what, ignored what your body, your mind, has been telling you? This husband of yours doesn't sound like much of a prize. He's not noticed your struggle? Not cared to fix it for you?"

Rushing to his defense, Zari raised her voice. "No, he has! He has, Nan. He has tried over and again to make me go to the doctor. He thought I might have a brain tumor."

Pop snorted. "Well, and we see what this has gotten you. You've tried to force your heritage to the side, and now look how sick you are!"

"I'm *sick* because of the shit Nan pulled on me! I was doing perfectly fine until she showed up in my dreams and tried to kill me! Wait…wait. Is this a dream? It feels so real." Hoping against hope, Zari clung to the possibility.

"It's not a dream. You're here, with us," he said, curtly.

"But where's Emmett? Why can I hear him?" she asked, confused.

"Because he's with you, just not here."

She shook her head in bewilderment. "I don't...I...?"

"Two realities, love. You're here, with us. And you're there with Emmett, at the hospital. You're in a coma." Pop was losing patience with her, she could tell.

Zari stared at the ceiling, contemplating the words, tossing them around in her mind, stretching them out like taffy.

"I don't care what I supposedly am. There is no way I can be two places at once," she said finally.

"Believe what you want, kid." Mama's voice was acid. "You're there, with your simpering excuse of a husband. And you're here, clearly, with us. "

"Am I going to die?"

"Your choice," Pop said, flatly.

Zari was screaming again, her already raw wrists wriggling in her bonds. "It's *not* my choice! None of this is my choice!"

The pain was immediate and hot. Pop's smack across her face was hard and unrestrained. The strike left first white then red prints on her skin. His voice devoid of emotion, cautioned her, "Zari. We've tolerated your nonsense long enough. You *will* agree to stay here. You *will* agree to accept Slither. And you *will* feed: for yourself, for your family, for the whole." Pop crouched down low and leaned in so that he was nose to nose with his rebellious daughter. "I know you understand me. Pledge your allegiance to Slither now or suffer the consequences." His voice was chilling.

"And if I don't?"

"Then you die. And so does Emmett. See, it *is* your choice." He smiled.

Arching up with her neck and shoulders as far as she was able, Zari looked directly into her father's gray-green eyes, so like her own.

"Fuck. You," she said precisely, and spat in his face.

~***~

At the house.

It was dark outside. It'd been dark all day, but night had fallen and the blackness was now thicker and heavier. Heat and humidity had risen to an almost intolerable level outside and in the house the air sat stale and palpable. There was no wind to relieve them, no breeze through the windows to cool their skin or ease their minds. Instead, the group shuffled between the kitchen and the living room, keeping candles lit and juggling hope like precious china plates.

"Do you think he made it?" The words came from Jessa.

Mr. Grady spoke up, his voice sure. "Of course he did. Emmett seems quiet, but he's a determined fellow. He'll have gotten to that hospital if he had to hitch a ride."

"Do you think Zari will make it?" Jessa asked, her voice low and trembling.

"I got faith." He nodded, pressing his lips together.

"Mr. Grady, do you pray?" The question popped out, surprising Jessa even as she heard the words blurt from her mouth.

"I do. Maylie and me both do."

"And you think it works?"

"Works? Well, prayer isn't a button we push to get just what we want." He snapped his fingers, "Like *that*. But we ask, and if our prayer is His will, it works out. If it isn't, He's in that, too, helping us through. We trust."

Jessa's voice broke. "But I don't…I don't want Zari to die. She's my best friend."

"We all want her to make it, Jessa. Until we know different, let's believe she's all right," he said, his voice strong and soothing.

"Food's ready!" Miss Maylie's strong voice belted from the kitchen. This was the fourth meal she'd made for them – it was fortunate the stove was gas – and they all rose from the various places they'd been sitting in the living room and walked with somewhat unwilling steps to sit at the table, Livvie carrying Iris on her hip. None of them were hungry, really. Their collective appetites had been lost after the events of the morning. Fear and stress filled their bellies already, but the truth was that Miss Maylie was a formidable presence and the girls were a little bit afraid of her. James had simply been conditioned to come to the table and eat when called after nearly a half a century of doing so.

Maylie muttered as she busied herself setting bottled water near each bowl. "No beef vegetable beef soup. Never heard such a thing in my life." Disgust was evident in her tone.

"Now Maylie," James chided. "You know Zari doesn't eat meat."

She mumbled as she sat her considerable rump down in her

seat. "Yes. Well. Maybe her poor husband wouldn't be so darn skinny if she made him a good meal now and again." She made a noise that sounded like 'harumph.'

"Maylie! Poor girl is sick and we don't know what all, don't you talk bad about her like that. And Emmett does eat meat. Just Zari don't. Be good, now." He raised his brows with a chiding expression on his face.

Maylie sniffed and clenched her jaw. "Pass the bread, will you?" James picked up the loaf from the center of the table and dropped it about a foot away from Maylie, making her have to stand back up in order to reach it. Maylie scrunched her nose and squinted.

Livvie and Jessa met one another's eyes off and on through the candlelight during this exchange. Neither dared to utter a word. Iris opened her mouth and shut it repeatedly, until Livvie scooped up some soup with her spoon, drained the broth off and fed the baby a bit of vegetable.

Jessa ate her soup in silence, the picture of Emmett's back still frighteningly clear in her mind. Hesitant but curious, Jessa worked to frame her question properly. "Mr. Grady, did you know about Emmett's..."

James stood abruptly, raising a hand to quiet her. "Listen." He tipped an ear toward the open window. "The wind is picking up out there." Howling, swirling winds had come out of nowhere, bending tree branches and hurling spiteful chunks of rain at the house. Something was wrong. "Maylie, you and the girls get back downstairs. I got a feeling..." No more had the words left his mouth than the siren wail began, rapidly rising in decibel. "Go, go, *go!*"

SLITHER

Mr. Grady moved along the exterior walls, slamming and locking windows then grabbing up the flashlights in his arms and blowing out the candle flames as he went. Heaven help them, he thought, as he moved toward the basement door. He'd survived some frightening weather in his lifetime, but two solid days with storms of this magnitude was unsettling even for his steel nerves. "Rocko! Come on, now. Come to daddy." Obedient, the dog lumbered over and followed his master. Balancing the flashlights in his left arm and reaching for the basement door knob with his right hand, James took a second to look back before he slammed the door shut and headed down. But without the candle flames, all he could see was utter and absolute blackness.

"James? James! Are you coming?" Maylie's voice was plaintive. "We're back in the utility room."

"I'm coming, Maylie. I'm coming. Ain't as fast as I used to be, you know."

As he neared the small room in the basement, he could hear the women fussing and moving around. Iris was shrieking at all the jostling around. "Just get under there with the baby." That was Jessa, he could tell. Then Livvie's voice, "I will. I mean, I am. Hush, Iris. Hush." Livvie felt sick as the pitch of the baby's screams grew louder, as if her crying could somehow alert the storm of where to find them.

James stepped inside the utility room and closed the door, beaming his little flashlight around the room looking for the seat he'd had yesterday. Maylie lumbered down beneath the table, followed by Jessa. James sat on his chair and rubbed his tired eyes as they listened to the raging storm over the baby's hysterical crying. "Hush, hush, hush," Livvie repeated uselessly, patting the baby's back as they crouched in the tiny space. Several moments had passed in measured chaos and the sounds of the storm seemed to invade the basement, whistling through the ears of the occupants in a painfully high tone. Each of them cringed or turned their faces in the darkness to somehow retreat from it, but the whining, hissing sound only grew louder.

"What *is* that?" Jessa blinked against the sound, covering her ears with her hands.

"It's gonna pull the roof off! It's gonna pull the roof off!" Maylie was shouting to be heard over the noise.

"Let's just all calm down for a minute!" Mr. Grady's baritone rose over the panicked sopranos.

Livvie spoke in an irritated tone. "Look, Jessa, I'm freaked out too, but please don't touch me like that."

"Like what? I'm not touching you!" Offended, Jessa pulled her head back a bit and scrunched her face.

"Seriously. I can feel you touching my ass. I don't know what your deal is, but I'm not..." said Livvie, with the flattened voice of someone quite used to having to deflect unwanted sexual attention.

"God! Livvie, I am *not* touching your ass! Why would you think that?"

"Because! You're next to me, and I can feel fingers..."

"What. The. Hell. *Dude.* Are you touching *me* now?" Jessa squealed, quickly crawling out from under the shelter of the table.

"Holy hell. I can still feel it. Mr. Grady, can you shine that light over here?"

Four pair of eyes focused on the space beneath the table. Four mouths opened in horrified screams at the sight that greeted them.

The floor was covered in snakes.

Disgusting black, slimy, writhing snakes.

Chapter Six

Revelation.

"Who in the world am I? Ah, that's the great puzzle."

— *Lewis Carroll, Alice in Wonderland*

Emmett.

Steve came returned to the room backward, shoving the door open with his right shoulder, a hot Styrofoam cup of coffee in each hand. His slow steps were just one indicator of his immense fatigue, and his heart filled with something he couldn't quite put his finger on as he looked at Emmett whispering to his wife. Jackson cleared his throat. Twice.

"Mr. Delaney. Er, Emmett, rather. Brought you something."

"Oh. Hey." Emmett reached up and took the cup in hand. "Thanks." He took a sip and flinched. Coughed. "God. That's terrible. Sorry."

"I know. Still, though. It's hot and the caffeine does its job. How're you feeling?" Steve asked.

"Headache's a bit better," said Emmett, obviously exhausted.

"Good. Feel up to talking some more? I'd like to get a more complete history on Mrs. – um, on Zari."

Emmett sat straighter in his wheelchair and replied, "Sure. What do you need to know?"

Steve was dragging over a muted gray chair, the chrome of the legs emitting an unwilling screech at the movement. Emmett winced slightly at the sound. Plopping the seat down on all fours and sitting down in it in one long, fluid motion, Steve propped his right ankle over his left knee – a move that showed off his surprisingly bright rainbow striped socks — and pulled a notebook and ink pen from his jacket pocket. "Yes. Right. Let's get started, then. Where were we? Oh, yes. Yes." Emmett sat quietly, waiting. "You'd mentioned the tremors and nightmares. Anything else unusual come to mind while I was gone? Anything you can think of might help us get Zari well again."

Emmett opened his mouth, closed it, pressed his lips together.

"What is it? Tell me," insisted the doctor.

"Well, I mean, yesterday, she was acting kind of strange. But you know, she's not a terribly typical woman. What I mean is, acting unusual is sort of usual, for Zari." He stopped, feeling that he wasn't able to explain himself properly. Emmett stared at his hands for a moment.

Nodding, Steve encouraged him to continue. "Strange, how do you mean?"

"I don't know if it's anything, really. But she was at work yesterday, and a storm came through the area. She had her car there but she *ran* the three miles home. I'm an English professor and my students have been, well, this week has been chaotic at work, to put it mildly. I got home from work and took a nap, and the next thing I knew Zari was in the bed, slapping at me and screaming for me to wake up. Scared the shit out of me, too. She seemed absolutely frantic. Said it looked like I wasn't breathing."

He reached back to rub his neck. "Then a little while later I was downstairs grading papers and she said she wanted to talk, then she refused to have a conversation beyond what to eat for dinner. I don't know where that all was going, but she seemed upset and I'm not sure why. She got all jumpy, we had a little bit of an argument, then I noticed she was shaking again. Her hands were trembling so bad, she dropped a can of soup."

"Hhmmnn. So let me ask you this, does it seem to you that the tremors are worse during times of stress, such as when the two of you are arguing?" In his mind, he was sorting through files of information, attaching symptoms to possible diagnoses; discarding those that seemed irrelevant, mentally highlighting anything that seemed germane.

"No. Well, I mean, I don't know. We don't argue often. Our relationship is solid. But she has seemed a little bit off, lately. And the last few months, the nightmares have been bad. *Really* bad. I have a difficult time waking her up from them, she just…." His voice took on a shaky quality of its own. "Like she looks so pale, and she screams and kind of, I don't know, makes these little sounds like she's hyperventilating or something. And her eyes, she's asleep but her eyes are open and Zari looks like she's seeing something so terrifying. I want to take it away and I can't, and the helplessness of that, I can't even tell you how impotent it makes me feel." Emmett balled his hands into fists, the blue lines of veins popping to the surface of his forearms.

"I can imagine. And how long do these episodes last?" Jackson was scribbling in his notebook.

"Oh, long time. The last one was at least two hours."

"Two *hours*? You're sure about that?" Steve paused and

looked up, his pen wavering above the paper.

"Yes. Look. I know that sounds terrible, and I've tried to get her to go to the doctor about it, but you just don't understand how incredibly stubborn she is. I mean, I love this woman more than my own life, but forcing her to do something she's opposed to doing is like smashing concrete with a straw."

Steve chuckled. That sounded familiar. He blinked away a sudden vision of Caroline.

"I'm not judging you, Emmett. But two hours seems like an unreasonable length of time for a nightmare to last, especially one such as you describe. I wonder if something else might be going on there, so we're going to go ahead and get a CAT scan and an EEG done. Continue." As he spoke, Steve jotted down words in his notebook.

"I...I just can't even think of anything else. I'm sort of scatterbrained. But I would have paid better attention if I had known..." Guilt tore at his insides, clawed fingers struggling for grip on a cliff. Emmett's voice deepened as emotion rose to the surface once again. He leaned forward, elbows on knees and face in his hands. His great shoulders shook as grief overtook him. "I didn't know. I didn't know this was going to happen. I should have tried harder."

"Emmett. Listen. You are not at fault here. Sometimes these things just happen, man. You've got to try and pull yourself together here. Focus. That's what's going to help your wife."

Nodding into his hands, he sucked hard at the air. "I know. I know. I know. Yeah."

"I've got another question for you. We noticed when Zari

first came in, she had a laceration on the back of her head that had bled quite a bit. Enough that her hair was matted with blood in that area. Have you any idea how that happened?"

The guarded personality was back in a flash. Straight shoulders, straight spine. Raised chin. Eyes blazing. "Now listen to me, Steve. You're talking about my *wife*. If you're suggesting I would *ever* lay a hand that woman, well, you couldn't be more mistaken." Furious, Emmett shot his long body up from the wheelchair, instantly regretting it as darkness speckled with bright, colorful lights consumed his vision; a spinning, dizzying Mobius strip he was unable to debark. Stubborn as his wife, he remained upright. And angry.

Steve had stood just as quickly and reached his arm out, worried the guy was going to topple over again. By the way Emmett swayed in place, that wasn't an altogether unfounded idea.

"Calm down. I wasn't…"

"Weren't you? Weren't you just suggesting I *hit my wife?*" His tone was decidedly acerbic.

"Actually, no. I wasn't. I'm sorry if it came out that way. Listen, buddy. Sit back down. Let's talk." Alarmed by the rapidly draining color in Emmett's face and his unfocused eyes, Jackson tried to remain calm. "Emmett? *Emmett!*"

Emmett's mouth opened but the words seemed swallowed up in the buckling of his knees.

Steve's voice was tired. "Well, shit. Here we go again."

This time, at least, Jackson managed to get his arms firmly beneath Emmett's armpits and was able to guide him down to the floor, though he struggled to do so gently. Thinking Emmett must have stood up too fast after such prolonged sitting, Jackson assumed he'd wake up after a moment. But after two minutes had passed, he became a bit more concerned and took a closer look. Emmett's hair was damp and his thin blue gown was developing a wet spot across the chest. Thumbing up his eyelids, Jackson found the pupils dilated and skin clammy. Pulse 115. Tachycardic. Quickly arranging his stethoscope, Jackson leaned over Emmett's chest and concentrated. Something was wrong with this guy and it wasn't simple stress and dehydration. Reaching up, Steve fumbled around Zari's still body until he located the emergency call button and pressed. In seconds, the room was filled with medical personnel: rushing, prodding, checking, counting. Jackson barked out instructions as the well-oiled hospital machine did its work. "…and I want an EKG on him, STAT! Another set of blood gases, and a CAT scan." The doctor leaned down to pick up the cup of coffee Emmett had dropped and spilled when he'd fainted. "And I need maintenance in here with a mop to clean this mess up."

Jackson stood staring at the brown liquid, the spreading spot a mirror of the fogginess his own brain felt at the moment.

"…isn't it though?" A veteran nurse with short, spiky brown hair and several decades of seasoning behind her was shaking her head as Emmett was wheeled out the door on a gurney.

Jackson shook his head, focusing with great effort. "I'm sorry, I didn't quite catch what you said there."

"I just said, you know, his wife in here already and as sick as he looks right now, that poor little cutie is having a rough time of it."

Nodding, Jackson latched onto and stuck to that one word,

"cutie", and wondered why. *Cutie.* Cutie. He mentally ran the word through brain files and came up short. He stood there in the near empty room and formed the word with his mouth, whispering it. His own voice reverberated in his ears. Cutie. Cu-tie. Kew-tie. QT. *QT.* His head snapped up and he slapped his hands together as he strode over to Zari and her chart. Long QT Syndrome! Why hadn't he seen it before? Yes, yes. He flipped through the chart, nodding, agreeing with himself. The horrendous nightmares, those could be seizure related, as could the slight personality changes Emmett had noticed. Long QT could also have stopped her heart, leaving her in this condition. Usually, once the heart stopped, that was it – but perhaps the quick response with CPR had kept her going. Winding up in a coma wasn't something he'd heard of, really, but he'd heard tales stranger than that happening in medicine. An electrocardiogram would be the first thing to get done and Jackson had no doubt it would prove his theory. He'd get her started on some beta blockers immediately, and hopefully with treatment plus faith and luck, Zari would make a turn for the better. Now, to figure out what the hell was wrong with Emmett. Something wasn't right, there. The first time he'd gone down, Jackson had assumed it was a combination of stress and dehydration; indeed, with some rest and IV fluids, he had seemed to be perking up. However, this second collapse couldn't be so easily explained away. Nothing to do for these two, now, just wait on test results. Jackson stood, weary to the bone and with an ache for Caroline so deep in his gut he placed his hand over his stomach and held it there for a moment. It was funny, how the pain could strike that way sometimes out of nowhere, fast and white hot. Jackson brushed at his white coat and straightened his tie, walking from the room. Three other patients to check in on – patients who weren't getting nearly the level of concentration from him as Zari and Emmett were. Oh, they were being well-cared for, certainly.

He was aware of their problems and test results and treatment plans, but he had one of his fellows stopping in to check in on them and make any decisions she deemed reasonable. With a weight in his step, Steve suppressed a yawn as he propelled himself toward the nurse's station. He'd just do a quick read-through of those charts and maybe curl up on the couch in the physician's lounge for a nap. A glimpse at his watch reminded Jackson he'd been awake for twenty-two hours and couldn't begin to think what he'd last eaten. Shutting the door to the blanket warming oven, he pulled two toasty white blankets around his shoulders like a cloak and sat down on the couch, slowly dragging himself flat on his back with his right leg bent. He felt heavy and old and somewhat jetlagged and his dead wife's face was there behind his eyelids waiting for him. He missed her lovely face. Her arms around him in bed. Her hair tangled in his hands. He just missed *her;* he missed Caroline. Jackson drew the blankets tighter around his body in an effort to ward off the chill that always arrived with the waves of grief. It never helped but he did it every time, just the same.

~***~

Zari

"What's happened? What have you done?" Zari's whisper to her mother was fierce, a sizzling shot of lightning in cold water.

"I've done nothing to you, kid. I don't know what you're talking about. Just calm down. Pop and Nan will be back soon, and then…"

"But that's exactly it, Mama! Please, just tell me before they get back in here. Tell me what they've done with him. I have to know!" said Zari, panic striking her features.

"Done with who? I honestly don't know what you're talking about." Her face was blank.

Zari stared at her mother intently. Mama was a liar and that was something Zari had always known inherently, the way other children knew their mothers were singers or artists or able to bake the best chocolate chip cookies. Thing was, Zari had never been able to crack the 'tells', those little things she could easily recognize in other people when they lied to her face. Mama didn't consistently clear her throat or touch her ear or look sideways toward the floor and it made it impossible to figure if she was saying something straight out or not.

"He's gone, Mama. Emmett's gone." Her lower lip wavered, and she bit it with her two front teeth.

"You crazy, kid? That man was never here. He's still with you, over at the hospital. Pop wouldn't allow him here." Mama looked at Zari as if she'd suddenly sprouted three extra heads.

"No, but Mama, listen. I could feel his presence, I could hear him whispering to me. I could feel his hand on mine, the heat of his hand, I could feel it, Mama." She was losing it again, her voice beginning to hiccup as she fought back hysteria. They were never going to let her go. They were going to kill Emmett. What if they already had? Why couldn't she feel him anymore?

"No, Zari. He would have told me if…he would have told me." There was strange tightness in Mama's voice. Almost like pity, but that couldn't be right.

Frantic, Zari squirmed and fought against her restraints, tearing the fragile scabbed skin that had only begun to form. Blood dripped with thick, dark drops back down the sides of her arms and onto the floor. "Mama. Take these things off of me."

"No. You'll run," said Mama, her tone brooking no argument.

"How can you do this to me? I'm your daughter, for God's sake!" Zari doubted guilt would help her case at all, but it was worth a shot at this point. Anything was.

"How could you turn your back on me and leave? How could you walk away from your family?" And there it came, the guilt had been caught and tossed right back at her like a Frisbee.

"Mama. You know why."

"We aren't bad people, Zari. If you would just embrace what you are, you'd see. It's not as terrible as you imagine it is. Feeding is an amazing thing. You'll feel so light, like you're floating above everything, not a single care to drag you down. You'll be happier if you just accept your purpose."

"Happy? You've never been happy. None of you. You've been miserable your entire life and you know it." Rather desperately, Zari wished she could take hold of her mother's shoulders and shake her. Hard.

"That's enough. My bouts of melancholy have nothing to do with Slither. Feeding saves me when I can't save myself. Surely you understand that. I cannot help my temperament. And you're cruel, throwing such a thing in my face. But then, you've always been selfish and mean that way."

Manipulation. Typical Mama. Her perpetually hunched shoulders and soured expression were accurate indicators of her personality.

Footsteps in the hall struck thudding anger in Zari's heart and she snapped her face toward the doorway, where Pop and Nan had appeared. "What. Did. You. Do?" Her words bit through the air like the snaps of a crocodile jaw.

Forehead to mouth, Nan's face was all smirk. "Whatever do you mean, child?"

"You know exactly what I mean! I want to know what has happened to my husband and I want to know *now!*" shouted Zari. Her already husky, throaty voice had deepened with fear.

"Emmett is fine. Calm down," said Nan, in a bored tone.

"He is not fine! I can't feel him with me anymore! If you killed him, Nan, I swear to God I will murder each of you, slowly and with great pleasure, I promise." Zari curled her trapped and bloodied hands into fists, clenching her teeth and baring them in a look that was anything but a smile.

Nan chuckled and rolled her eyes. "She's going to kill us. Oh no. I'm terrified." She walked across the room and leaned over Zari, bending down until she was merely an inch from her face. "Listen to me, little girl. Your husband is not dead. He is quite ill, however, and if you wish to prevent his imminent death you will obey. Fealty to Slither is your only chance to save him, though even in that you will still lose him. But he will live. Now," Nan hissed and droplets of spittle rained down on Zari's face, "let me make something perfectly clear to you. Threaten me, or any of us again and I will slice your head right off your body without so much as a smidgeon of guilt. Am I clear, Zari Uadjit?"

Flinching at the sound of her full given name, Zari ground her teeth. "What do you mean, he's ill?"

"Emmett is weak and having a bit of heart trouble at the moment. He will recover when you make the right decision. You want him to recover, don't you? As much as you claim to love him?" Nan was smug; she knew Zari was backed into a corner, now.

"I want...I want to go home *with* my husband!" Zari lifted her legs up in the air and slammed them down hard on the pallet. Childish, perhaps, but she was decidedly lacking ways to make her feelings known. And kicking felt good.

"That isn't going to happen, child," said Nan, a caustic flavor to her words.

"*Please!* I'll do anything!" Desperation was evident in her face.

Nan and Pop shared an intense look, words like an invisible thread passing between them. Pop nodded and glanced at Mama, squinting. Zari watched the exchange, her heart dropping as they communicated without her. She bit at her bottom lip and yanked her wrists up and down in the restraints. *Bastards could be planning to take off my head right now!* Sickening, sour acid filled her mouth at the thought. Panic set in, causing her teeth and bones to chatter.

Pop turned to her, and she remembered times long, long ago when his eyes weren't deadened and he didn't have such a grim set to his face.

"*Anything?* Be cautious what you say, Zari. Do you really mean that?" he asked, staring intently at her face.

Hope rose in her belly, impossible but something to grab onto nonetheless. She held it tight.

"Yes! Yes. Anything, Pop." Sweat dripped from her skin, even as she shook with chills.

"In that case, listen carefully. We will allow you to go – permit you to go back to your home, and allow you and your husband to live. Slither will absolve itself of you, provided…"

"What? Provided, what?" Eager for any way out, it was on her lips to agree before even hearing the conditions.

"Provided you give it to us and never come back," Pop finished.

Confused, Zari's eyes darted to each family member for clarification.

"I…I don't understand. Give you what, exactly?" she asked, cautiously.

"Why, the baby, of course."

~***~

At The House

"Oh my God! I hate snakes!" Jessa's screams rivaled the blustering gusts of wind surrounding the house, echoing through the walls. Rocko joined in with a baritone howl. Livvie had bolted from the infested utility room with Iris, and Miss Maylie was moving behind them at a pace that belied her age and arthritis. Pressed up against the stairwell, the trio was attempting to catch their collective breath. The shuddering in Maylie's chest begged to be formed into a scream, but her breathing was still too short and shallow for that. Iris continued to cry at the top of her lungs, only adding to the cacophony of misery and terror. Mr. Grady slapped gently at Jessa's arm. "Get out there!" he whispered, pointing to the door. Caught between the desire to run and grim resolve insisting she somehow rectify the situation, Jessa scanned the room for ideas. Her eyes fell on a familiar jug shape on the table. "Mr. Grady, shine the flashlight over here." Exactly as she'd thought – it was bleach. Gingerly, she stepped within the few bare patches between the writhing masses on the floor. Grabbing the bottle in one hand and yanking the lid off with the other, she poured the liquid on the repulsive crowd of hissing snakes. Immediately, the hissing sound rose in pitch to a nearly deafening level along with smoke and an acidic burning stink that left the occupants of the basement holding their breath and covering their noses and mouths. Finally, the basement was quiet – even Iris had quieted her crying. Singed, crumbled chunks of snakeskin littered the floor of the utility room. "I'm going to puke," Jessa announced, leaping from where she stood through the doorway in one jump. She stood in the center of the dark space and crossed her arms over her lurching stomach. Mr. Grady stepped out, silent, and closed the door on the mass of death in the small room.

~***~

Emmett

"He's looking better, getting a little color back." Jackson's eyes flitted from one machine to another. "I don't think the oxygen is necessary, so let's get that off him. He's got a bit of an issue with feeling tied down. I don't want him to wake up and start yanking things apart again. Only the absolute necessities, please." One nurse turned off the oxygen and removed the cannula while the second pressed flashing buttons on the machine hooked to the IV pole. Three hours since he'd passed out again, and Jackson was confident he would wake soon. The doctor hadn't quite figured out what was causing the guy to keep having these little episodes, but at any rate his glucose was back up to a decent level and his blood pressure and tachycardia had stabilized. Zari, on the other hand, was worsening. Long QT syndrome explained most of her symptoms except the bruises along her forearms and wrists that had appeared out of nowhere. He'd ordered another round of labs, this time to check for anemia, von Willebrand, and vitamin K deficiency. The first round of labs had already come back and as Jackson checked them over, he stared hard at one result in particular. Oh boy. He wanted to be the one to tell Emmett when he woke up. If things didn't start moving in a positive direction for Zari, Emmett was going to have some difficult choices to make.

"Kate," Jackson said to the remaining nurse, "any sign he is starting to wake, page me immediately. Got that?"

"Yes, doctor."

"I'm heading down to the cafeteria. Page if you need me."

~***~

Chicken salad. Again. Biggest hospital in the county and you'd think they could come up with more variation than the standard chicken salad, chocolate cake and mashed potatoes and gravy that filled the dishes beneath the sneeze guards. Steve plopped some of each selection on his plate and slid his orange plastic tray up the metal counter to the cashier. Once paid, he made his way to an out-of-the-way booth and sat with his back to the crowded eating area. Three bites of a sawdust dry chicken salad sandwich and two bites of mashed potatoes into his meal, his pager started beeping. Standing and stepping over to the trash can, he emptied his tray into the refuse container – but not before shoving the entire slice of chocolate cake into his mouth. Stepping through the elevator doors and pressing the correct floor button, Steve thought about the best way to approach Emmett with the information he now had.

~***~

Emmett groaned at the intensity of pain in his head and back. Panic again pricked at him, a buzzing, icy sensation in his gut as he realized, once again, he was hooked to various machines and had another IV in his arm. But the frantic feeling subsided a bit when he saw Zari in the bed next to his. He blew out a long, hard breath, trying to force himself to relax. At least they were in the same room this time. He felt around for the buttons on the bed and once located, helped himself to a sitting position as he took stock of the situation. The room was painfully stark and devoid of color. Emmett thought about how stark his life would be if Zari didn't wake up. But she had to. She *had* to. He blinked rapidly. Of course she would wake up. The fluorescent lights were a strain on his eyes and he squinted. His head and back hurt and throbbed something fierce but other than that, he didn't feel too terrible. The hospital had a lingering stain in the air that smelled of urine and stale gravy and he crinkled his nose at it, wishing they could spray something in the room that would take it away. He was considering some questions he wanted to ask Steve when the man himself walked into the room, meeting Emmett's eyes with a nod as he picked up his chart. They both spoke at the same time.

"Steve, what in the hell…"

"Emmett. We need to talk."

"What happened? Why do I keep passing out like this? It's never happened to me before."

"Well, buddy, that's what we're trying to figure out. Have you ever had a problem with tachycardia – ever felt like your heart was beating too fast or too hard?"

Emmett shook his head slowly. "No, why? Is that the problem with me?"

"One of them. Your blood sugar tanked again and so did your blood pressure. All your tests haven't come back yet, so I'm still trying to get it figured out. But while we wait I want to talk to you about Mrs. Del – about Zari."

Ice immediately clinched Emmett's stomach and he leaned forward, a furrow deepening between his brows. "What's this now?"

"She's shown no signs of waking up, and she's got some rather horrific bruises on her arms. Does she usually bruise easily or seem as if she bleeds too much when she gets cut? Are her periods overly heavy?"

"Ahhh…she's never mentioned her periods being too heavy," Emmett flushed slightly at the privacy of the statement, "I know her cycles tend to be irregular. I don't know that she…well, you know earlier. Well, yesterday? She ran into the utility room to change her clothes during the storm, and slipped and fell. She hit her head pretty hard – that's how she got that cut and bloody dreads. It did seem like it bled hard for quite a while."

"I'm testing her for several bleeding disorders, but it looks like she has long QT syndrome as well. Have you ever heard of that?"

"No. Tell me." Hungry for knowledge of the threat, Emmett leaned forward. If he could understand the threat, he could fight it.

Somehow.

"It's a genetic heart condition that causes an irregular heartbeat. It can cause fainting, even cause the heart to stop all together. I think that's what happened with Zari, and you just woke up, thank God, at the right time. "

"So is this condition fatal?" Emmett hiccupped on the last word. Twisted the thin blanket in his fist.

"It can cause death, but more often people spend their entire lives not knowing they have it until one day they have a big episode that ends in diagnosis. But Emmett, there is something else we need to talk about. "

Fear chilled him and Emmett stared hard at Steve's face, trying to read him. "What?"

"Look, I hate to be the one to tell you this, Emmett. But Zari is pregnant."

"She's *what*?" Startled, Emmett blinked hard and sat up straight.

"About three months."

"You're positive about this?"

"Absolutely."

Working to process the information, the unconscious finger tapping of his left hand began – repeatedly, Emmett touched each fingertip to his thumb, in order and back again. Jackson noticed it, but remained silent. What an odd little psychomotor agitation, he thought. Interesting. "She didn't say anything about it. Why wouldn't she tell me?"

"She may not have known, especially if, as you say, her cycles are irregular."

"And is...I mean, is it okay? The baby, I mean?" Emmett's jaw worked on one side, as though he was grinding the teeth together. A muscle twitched down the length of his jaw.

"As far as I can tell everything looks healthy as far as the pregnancy goes. But listen." Steve stopped and pulled the chair up to the bed, laying a hand on Emmett's arm. He squeezed. The lines around his eyes and mouth deepened as he spoke. "Emmett, Zari is not well. We've not seen anything that shows us she is getting better. Now she has new symptoms, the bruising. That isn't good. If we find out she has a bleeding disorder there may be a way to treat it, but I don't know that for sure just yet." He lowered his voice. "Emmett, you need to understand that your wife may not ever wake up. And if she doesn't, Emmett, if she doesn't then I need to know if you want to continue with this pregnancy."

"*What?* What are you asking me?" Emmett's voice was booming, echoing off the walls.

Steve remained calm, simply a physician listing options. However, he squeezed Emmett's arm as he spoke. "Terminating now is a viable option. And if she doesn't wake up that decision will be up to you."

"No. *No.* Don't do that. I don't...Zari wouldn't want that. I don't want that. If she's pregnant, then..." a great, gulping sob interrupted his words, "I want to try to keep the baby. Please." His fingers were moving incredibly fast now; the first finger tapping twice, with the rest in quick succession. Steve was rather medically fascinated with the oddity of Emmett's reaction.

SLITHER

"All right. We'll do all we can. But be prepared – the situation may change, Zari could get worse, and we may need to revisit this decision. You understand what I'm saying?" He spoke slowly, deliberately.

Emmett nodded. The finger tapping ceased. He sprawled his big hands out on the thin hospital blanket, spreading the fingers wide apart and pressing hard, as though the bed was an anchor and if only he could suction himself to it, the world would stop spinning. The skin of his fingers blanched, the lines of his knuckles accentuated in the fluorescent lights. Emmett crunched inward a bit, tucking his chin to his chest and blew out a harsh breath, working to center himself.

"Steve. Um…thanks for getting that scarf for her hair."

"No problem.

~***~

Zari

"The baby? What do you mean, the baby?" Her voice was small and as the words sank in and she began to understand them, she pressed her lower back down against the pallet; an instinctive and unconscious effort to draw the baby away from threat.

"You expect me to believe you didn't know?" Nan's smirk was condescending.

"I didn't! I didn't know! I can't give you my baby. Not Emmett's child."

"Not even to save your life? To save Emmett's life? The baby won't survive if you're dead. Or are you too stupid to understand even that? You cannot save all three of you. You and

Emmett can have another child."

"You can't expect me to just hand over my baby!" Panic rose within Zari, leaving her bones vibrating with terror.

"Please, you have no attachment to the little tumor. You didn't even know it existed until I told you."

"But now I do! I can't. I can't, Nan. Mama, please."

Mama shrugged weak, sweater covered shoulders, stringy hair in her face. "You could have another baby, Zari. And you won't cooperate with us and accept Slither. What can we do? You've made the situation impossible."

"*I've* made it impossible? I haven't done anything! If you would have just left me alone this wouldn't be happening!" Terror vibrated her voice and she shook her arms against the straps that held her, suddenly desperate to place her hands over her stomach. Nan had a particular penchant for stomping on Zari's abdomen as punishment for disobedience, and Zari recalled the agony of those instances quite vividly.

"Brat." This time, Zari saw Nan's hand coming toward her, but was powerless to stop it. *I am powerless to stop anything.* The slap was hard enough to knock her out cold for a few moments, and painful enough to have left a bright red handprint on her cheek.

"Never could do anything with this one. You should have beat her more when she was younger, made her submissive. I told you." Nan shot accusing eyes toward Mama's face.

Mama lowered her eyes, repentant. "You're right. I should have listened."

"No matter. We'll scrap her, keep the kid. Start all over."

Leaning against the wall in the corner of the room, Gianna smiled.

Chapter Seven

Chicken Salad Sympathy.

*"When one realises one is asleep,
At that moment one is already half-awake."*
— P.D. Ouspensky

Emmett

"...so what I'm doing here, Emmett, is I'm going to put this gel on Zari's belly, like this, and take a peek at the baby, see how things look. With any luck, we might be able to hear the heartbeat. No, now buddy, stay in the bed. Stay put. "Jackson held a hand up at Emmett. "I'll turn the monitor so you can see. Just give me a minute." Emmett fought against his own dizziness as he leaned forward in the hospital bed. Squinting, he pointed at his wife. "What's that on her face? Is it another bruise?"

Jackson stood and walked around the foot of the bed. "I'll be damned. It *is* another bruise. Would you look at that?" Gently, he slid the side of his thumb across the burgeoning mark on Zari's face. "I'm going to have to find out where her lab results are. I ordered them STAT, so they should have been here by now. But first, let's get this ultrasound done." Steve dragged the portable machine nearer Zari's lifeless body and held a large plastic wand in his hand, rubbing it over her belly. New beeping sounds mixed with the old ones, all sounding louder than the automatic whooshing of the machine that continued her robotic breathing. Steve watched the screen as he moved the device around, finally settling in one place, and pressed some buttons on the keyboard of the ultrasound machine. With a tired smile, he turned the monitor so Emmett could see it. "See this little peanut shape? That's your baby, Emmett. Now listen." Flipping on a switch near the keyboard, a loud, swishing sound filled echoed in the room. "That's the heartbeat. Sounds strong." Emmett slapped at his face as tears formed in his eyes. "My God. Our baby. I can't believe this is happening. I mean I'm...I'm scared to death. For Zari and now for the baby. But I feel something bubbling in my gut. Excitement, I think. I want to hold my child one day, Dr. Jackson. Please. Please find a way to save my wife." His words, like his face, were earnest.

"I'm doing as much as I can. I'm fighting for her, Emmett. You can believe that."

The need to connect with this man who held his wife's life in his hands was great. "Tell me...Steve, would you tell me about your wife, or girlfriend or...will you tell me what happened?"

Steve stood, sat back down, stood again. "I, uh, should really get on those test results." He cleared his throat.

"Please."

"Let me check out those lab results. I'll get us both another terrible coffee. And then I'll come back here and tell you about my Caroline. Okay?" It was going to be painful, and he knew it. But more agonizing was the thought that she might be forgotten, that her story would be gobbled up and lost in the sea of people who lived and cried and laughed and died every day.

"Okay."

Emmett lay back in the bed, exhausted and worried.

Rubbing his face, he contemplated the news he'd just absorbed. A baby. Zari was pregnant. He was going to be a father. Well, truly, he *was* a father. Starting now, he had to do his best for that child. *Their* child. Resolved, he sat up slowly, looking over at Zari. His eyes softened at the sight of her. She had to get better. They were going to be a family. Tenderness swelled within him, the warmth of it spreading through his gut, chest, and arms.

Once again, Steve stepped through the door backward, shoving it open with his shoulder as he held two coffee cups aloft, a bag with sandwiches dangling from his fist. "Hey, Emmett. Got some news on those test results, so let's talk about that first, okay?"

"Yeah." Emmett reached up for the cup and clasped his hand around it, feeling its warmth. "So, what did you find out?" He accepted the offered sandwich.

"It looks like she has Von Willebrand disease, but apparently type one, which is mild. We can give her more factor – I mean, the clotting factor she appears to be deficient in. If she is able to make it to term with this pregnancy, there could be complications, so we'll have to have her followed by a hematologist. But let's not get ahead of ourselves. We'll just take this one day at a time." He bit into his sandwich, chewing thoughtfully.

Emmett waited, nodding. *Tap-tap, tap, tap, tap* drummed his fingers.

"...so my wife, Caroline." He took a long sip of coffee. "We met when I was on a surgical rotation here at Mercy as a med student. She was a surgical nurse. Gorgeous. Confident. Smart. My heart was long gone before I ever asked her out for the first time. The way she walked, the way she carried herself, I could just imagine the kind of person she would be. I'd been watching her for a solid month before I worked up the courage to ask her out. She said no."

"She said no?"

"Yeah. Crushed me, man. Let me tell you. Said she didn't date coworkers. I asked her, what about when I move to the emergency room rotation? Would you date me then? She laughed and said to give her a call, then. So I did. We had a lot of dates in the cafeteria over terrible food. It wasn't as if I fell in love with her at any particular time, I don't think. There was just this easiness, this warmth, when we were together and an ache when we were apart. Our lives had become so intertwined, I couldn't imagine us separated, ever. So after a year, I asked her to marry me. She cried and said yes. And that was that. Twenty years passed in a blink. We built a home, built a life together. She started having pain in her right hip. Thought it was arthritis. Ignored it, until one day she couldn't. Osteosarcoma. I'm a doctor, for God's sake. I should have seen it. I should have..." Jackson drifted off for a moment, staring at the wall at something only he could see. "But I didn't. And it went so fast. She had the best physicians, I made sure of it. The best treatments. But her decline was quick and cruel. Her skin...her soft, white skin thinned like yellowed paper, until it seemed too fragile to touch. Her weight dropped, so fast. I made her eat, I cooked her favorite foods. Anything she wanted. But the cancer ate it all up. Caroline just wasted away. Infections plagued her and she couldn't fight them off. Her beautiful hair fell out. I used to tangle that hair in my hands and hold it." Steve held his hand out, staring at it. He cleared his throat again. "Anyway. It was a matter of months and she was gone. *Gone.* My wife. Some days I still can't believe it. That's it. That's my story. And Emmett, there's something in you, in the way you look at Zari, that reminds me of myself loving Caroline. And I want your story to end more happily than mine did."

Swallowing hard, Emmett whispered, "I'm sorry."

"So am I. Every day."

~***~

Zari

Pop rubbed his chin, thinking. "And you think this is the best course of action?"

Nan was confident. "Absolutely. She won't cooperate. She's said it herself. I say we let her go back to her husband, incubate our heir and when the time comes, we take the child. "

"And what of Zari and Emmett?"

"I see no reason they need to survive. Besides, she'll keep whining, coming after us to get the child back. You know how stubborn she is. We'll take the baby. Slay the parents. It's a simple plan, really."

"Yes, I agree. We know where we went wrong raising Zari. We can do better with the new child. Plans will need to be set on the back burner for now, but I believe in the end, Slither will be pleased."

"Indeed. Release her. Send her back. We'll get what we need in due time."

~***~

Emmett

SLITHER

He had just taken a bite of the chicken salad sandwich and chewed, watching as Steve adjusted the rate of the dripping liquid in his IV. His eyes were on Zari's belly, thinking of the baby, imagining how it would look, rounded with life. Drifting, he slid his gaze up her body, to her chest and its forced rhythmic breathing. Her long, slender neck. Her beautiful, gray-green eyes. Emmett jumped forward, dropping his sandwich on the floor and shouting at Jackson, "Steve! She's awake! Look!" Startled, Steve looked over at Zari and sure enough, her eyes were wide open. Terrified. Owlishly darting around the room. But still. She was awake.

"Zari, try to stay calm. My name is Dr. Jackson. You're at Mercy Park Hospital and you have a tube down your throat that is helping you breathe. Emmett is here. You are safe. If you understand what I'm saying, blink twice." With professional curtness, he pulled a pen-shaped light from the pocket of his white coat, flicking the light into her eyes, watching her pupils dilate and automatically reaching his opposite hand down to slip around her wrist, taking her pulse.

Blink. Blink.

"Babe? Babe, you're awake! Oh my God, I've been so worried..." His voice cracked, and he made to jump from the bed.

"Emmett. Emmett! Stay seated! Last thing I need at this moment is to have to scrape you off the floor again!" Steve's voice was clear. He would brook no argument. He tilted his head and raised his brows.

"I can't just—" His left hand was twitching; fingers frantically tapping.

"Yes, you can. Give me a minute to check Zari out, and I'll call a nurse to bring a wheelchair back in for you. "

"I love you, Zari. I love you! I'm right here, babe." His long legs dangled over the edge of the bed and he gripped the bedrail with a ferocity that left his knuckles unnaturally white. A nurse came running into the room and Jackson barked orders at her that she scrambled to obey. Next thing Emmett knew, several more nurses and two new doctors had invaded their space. "Excuse me. Can I get a wheelchair? Somebody? I want to see my wife." One of the nurses nodded at him but raised a finger. *Wait.* He fought for patience as he watched the slew of medical personnel prodding and poking his Zari, murmuring about readouts and numbers on the various machines. Minutes that felt like hours passed by and finally a nurse appeared at his bedside with a wheelchair. Cautiously, he slid down and into the uncomfortable seat and worked his feet on the floor until he reached her bed. Gentle and still a little afraid of hurting her, he took her hand in his and looked in her eyes, smiling. "I'm so happy you woke up, babe. It's going to be okay."

He's crying. Why is he crying? He looks awful. Pale, sweaty. Swollen eyes. Don't cry, love. I don't understand what's happening. Did they let me go? They wouldn't do that. Then how am I here? She curled her hand around his, despite the pain from the bruises on her wrists.

Jackson's voice broke between them. "We're going to extubate her, Emmett. See if she can begin breathing on her own. I don't think you're going to want to watch this."

"But I—"

"Just roll back to the other side of the room and pull the

curtain. I'll tell you when we're finished and you can come back over. Okay?"

It wasn't really a question, and Emmett knew it. He was being told to bugger off, and he warred within himself. He wanted to stay with her, hold her, protect her. But to watch them hurt her and to once again be helpless to stop it, made him feel ill. He kissed her hand. "I'll be right over there, babe. And I'll come back as soon as they let me. I promise." Emmett turned his face from her quickly. He pushed hard at the large wheels, propelling himself from the misery behind him. He felt decidedly weak.

The physicians murmured, busying themselves with the task at hand. Emmett listened as the machines quieted, and the movements of medical personnel seemed overly exaggerated in the previously still room. Gurgling, gagging sounds came from Zari, and Emmett imagined her arching up in the bed as they yanked the tube from her throat. He grimaced, his jowls filling with saliva at the thought of it. He sucked his cheeks in, letting the space between his teeth fill with the slick flabbiness of them, and bit down softly.

Finally, it was over. Jackson's haggard face was rough and worn as he came around the curtain and sat on the bed with Emmett. He patted Emmett's knee beneath the white blanket. "We'll have to monitor her closely for several days, but I think she'll be okay. She can't talk yet and you might hear stridor – a static-like, wheezing sound when she breathes. That's perfectly normal. Ready?" At Emmett's nod, Jackson helped him from the bed and into the wheelchair, pushing him over to Zari's side of the room.

Despite the obvious signs of illness still present, Emmett grinned at the sight of Zari without the tube and equipment around her face. The mechanical hum of the machine that had been making her breathe was now blessedly silent. Grimy, rectangular outlines from bandages left her with the look of an endearingly dirty waif, and the color of her eyes was accentuated by the dark gray smudges beneath them. Her parched lips had blanched to a very pale pink. A deep grumbling sound echoed through the room with each shaky breath Zari took, and Emmett shot his eyes at Jackson to double check this was the "normal" stridor sound he had spoken of. Jackson nodded.

"I want to talk with both of you for a minute about Zari's treatment plan, and then I'll leave you guys alone for a bit. Zari, as I've told Emmett, you've got a mild bleeding disorder called von Willebrand disease. It's nothing to be alarmed about, but we've started you on von Willebrand factor to help with the bruising you've been experiencing. We've also diagnosed you with long QT syndrome, which is a genetic condition that causes irregular heart rhythm and sometimes even stops the heart. Do you know of anyone in your family who has had a problem like that?" Wide-eyed, Zari shook her head, an almost imperceptible action – just a quick, partial shake to the right and back again. "Okay. Well, we're going to take good care of you, so don't worry overmuch about it. We think you had an episode that caused your heart to stop, but thanks to your husband and his quick response with CPR, I think you'll be okay. However, I want to start you on some beta blockers to help with the heart issue. Am I being clear?" One slow nod affirmed her understanding. "Good. Emmett tells me you're a vegan? Lack of potassium can also affect long QT syndrome, so I want you to really watch your diet, make sure you're getting enough. And until we're sure we've got it under control, I want you to try and avoid stressful situations. I know that sounds stupid. And I do realize we can't always avoid the things that upset us, but just try, okay? How long you remain here will depend on the results of a few more tests and how you do breathing just room air – we aren't going to try that just yet though, the oxygen will have to stay on a little while longer. Beyond that, I need to know you can eat and keep it down and we might try that tonight. Now, while you've been in La La Land, your husband has been passing out on us and experiencing an increased heart rate. At the moment, he seems to be doing okay as long as he doesn't try to stand up. I'm still trying to get that figured out, so the two of you may not be able to leave the hospital at the same time. For now, though, let's just focus on getting you both well again. Okay? I guess that's it. I know you two have a lot to talk about so I'll be back around in about an hour."

A hard lump sat in Emmett's throat as he stared at his wife. There was so much he wanted to tell her: how frightened he'd been when he'd found her not breathing and turning blue, how scary it had been to do CPR on her, how worried he'd been that she would die, and of course, the baby. He had to tell her about the baby. So many words pushed at his throat, insisting to be let out, but getting them past that damn lump felt impossible. He opened his mouth, shut it. Opened it again. Overwhelmed, Emmett leaned forward until his head lay on Zari's stomach, his hand stretched across her belly. She reached toward him until her hand connected with his head, and slipped her fingers through his messy, curly brown hair. Oh, how she'd missed that, the feeling of his thick hair sifting through her fingers. Zari closed her eyes, working to concentrate on breathing, on Emmett, on simply *being*. *I have to tell him. How can I even begin to explain this situation? They've hurt him, I can see that much. They might have let me go, but I know they'll be back. I should leave, to protect him. But I can't take the baby away from him. He's always wanted a child.*

Hiccupping sobs erupted from her, great, shaking gulps that

hurt her throat. There was no way to win. Stay with the man she loved more than her own life and risk the survival of all three of them. Leave Emmett, she'd be on her own with a baby and likely persecuted by her disgusting family with no way to fight back or keep her child safe. And even if she fled there was no guarantee they would leave Emmett alone. Hell, they might just kill him for the fun of it. She wanted Emmett and she wanted her baby and she wanted some way to get out of this mess but simply couldn't see a solution. "Don't cry, babe. Don't cry. It's okay. Everything's going to be okay now. Ssshhh." Emmett's voice was warm and loving. As far as he was concerned, their only obstacle was to get well and released from the hospital and everything would be fine. He sat up and gave her a lopsided smile, the sight of his crooked eyetooth at once filling and paining her soul. "The worst is over. You're awake. I was afraid I was going to lose you, but you're awake! You're breathing on your own! That's all that matters. And I need to tell you something, sweetheart. Listen, they were running all these tests on you and your bloodwork showed something surprising. Zari," Emmett sat up and looked at her, his eyes filled with seriousness. Gingerly, he took both her hands in his and kissed them. "You're pregnant. We're going to have a baby. Isn't it great?" His smile lit up his entire face and his expression pulled at her heart. *I love him so much. I will kill them if they try to take this away from us.* Determined to find a way to escape Slither and her family nightmare, Zari pulled her hand from Emmett's and slid folded fingers down the side of his face. "I love you," she mouthed. Together, they would figure out a way to separate from Slither and build their own life.

 The only problem now was how to explain to Emmett what, exactly, her family was.

 What *she* was.

But she had to tell him, and soon.

~***~

At the House

"Is it over?" Livvie's whisper was intended to not wake the finally sleeping Iris. The little girl was curled against her mother's chest, her round cheeks red from warmth and hours of screaming and her hair damp with sweat.

"I think so." Jessa's voice was cautious as she stood, stretching her back after hours spent crouched against the basement wall. She fisted her hand and rubbed her tailbone. "Look at them."

Mr. Grady and Miss Maylie were curled up together on the floor, with his back against the staircase and his arms around her. Rocko was sprawled out in front of the pair, the ever-present guardian. They'd been sleeping for hours.

"Livvie, I'm going to go upstairs and look around, see what's happening. You stay down here with Iris, just in case."

Quietly running up the steps on the balls of her feet, Jessa creaked the basement door open an inch at a time. Cocking an ear to listen, she heard nothing but a lone tree branch beating against the living room window so she walked up into the main floor of the house. Difficult as it was to see out of the windows in the darkness, Jessa squinted as she peered through the glass and crossed her arms over her chest to help ward off the chill in the room. More trees were down, both in the yard and the road. She could see the shadowed outlines in the black night outside. The wind had stopped and a soft rain was falling.

Valarie Savage-Kinney

The storm was over.

Chapter Eight

Homecoming.

*"But to me, so damn easy to see
That your people are the people at home
Well I been away, but now I'm back today
And there ain't a place I'd rather go."*
-Marc Roberge, *I Feel Home*

Four Days Later.

"Well, babe. We're heading home in style!" Emmett laughed as they bumped along in the back of the ambulance. The driver was working hard to maneuver past rocks, branches and other debris from the storms still in the road. Clean up had begun in the town, but it was slow going and country dirt roads – like where Emmett and Zari lived – were low priority. "I wonder if my truck got towed? We'll have to go out and look for it once we get everything settled."

"Yeah. I'm glad to go home." Zari's typically deep, throaty voice was barely more than a whisper, still damaged from the intubation. Still exhausted from the entire ordeal, a weak smile twitched the corners of her mouth. "I want my own bed."

"I bet you do. Sounds good to me, too. I wonder if everyone is still at our house, or if they've made their way home by now. These roads are still pretty bad. Mr. Grady might have gotten Livvie's car running, though. Power could still be out, too." He was prattling to settle his nerves and fill the time, and Zari recognized it for what it was and leaned in to him, pressing her head into his shoulder and draping her arm around his back.

"Love you."

"I love you too, babe." He kissed the top of her head. The ambulance lurched in a zig-zag around some obstacle and Emmett threw his free arm out to brace them from falling. "We should be getting close."

Ten minutes later, the ambulance braked hard and the pair stumbled from their seat in the back. "You all right?" Zari nodded. "I'll be so happy to get out of this rig." He looked up at the click of the outside handles, and the double doors at the back of the ambulance opened.

"Sorry about the rough ride," said the paramedic who'd offered to drive them out. "Couldn't be helped."

"It's all right. Thanks for bringing us home."

The paramedic reached a hand up to clasp Emmett's and helped guide him down from the vehicle. Zari crawled to the back of the rig and Emmett wrapped his arm beneath her armpits, holding her up as she carefully moved out and down. Together they stood in their driveway, surveying the damage. A tree trunk had completely smashed through the top of Jessa's car. Livvie's vehicle was right where it had been left, so clearly Mr. Grady hadn't gotten it up and running yet. Silhouettes moved around inside the house, so everyone must still be there, Emmett guessed. "Ready?" Zari smiled and nodded. Holding hands, they walked slowly up to the front door and stepped inside.

"Baby Girl! You're home!" The excitement on Mr. Grady's face was evident as he threw his arms out and walked toward them. Maylie was behind him, folding up the blankets and stacking them on the couch. Livvie had Iris on the floor, changing her diaper.

Jessa came running from the kitchen when she heard Mr. Grady's happy cries. Her eyes watered as she watched her friends come into the house.
Both of them looked pale and run down, but alive – although Zari had bruises all over her arms – and that was something that hadn't been a guarantee before right this moment. Jessa blinked rapidly as her eyes filled with water and her chin wobbled. "You're okay? You're both okay! Oh my God, we didn't know if…I mean, you went in the helicopter and you looked so bad, like you were *blue*, Zari! And Emmett just up and left so fast, we didn't know if he even made it to the hospital or not. I was afraid—" her voice trailed off. "I was afraid we'd lost you both." She dragged her arm across her wet eyes and waited for Mr. Grady's hug to end so she could grab Zari up in one of her own. "Come here. I missed you!"

Wrapping her arms around her friend, Zari whispered back, "I missed you, too."

"What's wrong with your voice?"

Zari looked up at Emmett to help with the explanation. "She was intubated – they shoved this tube down her throat to help her breathe. She won't have a voice beyond a whisper for a few days while everything heals up. So just try not to ask her to talk much, okay?"

"She's okay, though, right?" Jessa shifted her gaze back to Zari. "You're okay. You look good. Just tired."

I'm so tired. I could drop right here and sleep for days. Zari patted Jessa's back and staggered over to the couch. Emmett spoke up, "She needs to rest, guys. But we're happy to be back home, too. So fill me in on what's been going on around here. It doesn't look like the crews have made it out this way yet and the roads are still a mess. And, uh, Jessa...I'm sorry about your car."

"Yeah. Well. I'll figure something out. Hopefully something in my insurance policy covers freakish storm damage. I wonder what's going on at my house. For all I know, I don't even have a house anymore."

"I doubt mine's still standing. We just have a little singlewide trailer in that trashy park over on Morrison Road." Livvie's eyes were downcast as she stood and started bouncing the baby on her hip. After seeing the scars on Emmett's back the other day, she felt uncomfortable looking him in the eye. "I hope it's not gone. It isn't much, but it's our home. I don't have anywhere else to go."

"What is it you do, Livvie?" This from Mr. Grady, as he watched Maylie unfold a multicolored quilt to lay over Zari, who'd already fallen asleep on the couch.

"Right now, I'm a full time nursing student at the university. I'm trying to get into a better situation for us. I only have six months of classes left then I can start my clinicals."

"Good for you! That's great. Keep it up!"

"Yeah. Thanks." She blushed. Livvie hated the situation she'd brought Iris into. Livvie's mother had all but disowned her, and Iris' father had bolted before the baby had even been born. But she was trying to make better decisions and build a good life for her little girl. "I've screwed up a lot. But I'm focused on the future. No matter what, the best thing for Iris is what's most important."

"She's lucky to have a mama like you." Maylie's voice was soft and tender, a startling variation from her usual brusque bark. Livvie ducked her head and smiled.

"I'm doing the best I know how to do. I love her so much," Livvie put a fist toward her heart, "Iris means all the world to me. I'd die for her."

"Of course you would. That's how any good parent feels."

Zari had dozed off but woke in time to hear the exchange between Livvie and Maylie. She dropped her hand down to her stomach and pressed against it. *I'd die for you if it came down to it. But first, I'd kill to protect you.* Zari imagined the little one inside: a tiny peanut growing into a perfect baby and she felt warm and happy all over. Reaching up toward Emmett, she motioned for him to bend down nearer her face. "Tell them," she mouthed. Emmett didn't need to be asked twice. He was so incredibly proud he felt as if he might burst with the joy of their secret. "Hey, guys? Listen. Zari and I, we want to tell you all something. While we were in the hospital, we found something really exciting out." He smiled down at Zari and looked back at the group. "We're going to have a baby!" Squeals and claps filled the room and Mr. Grady walked over to hug Zari again and clapped Emmett on the back. "Couldn't be prouder for you kids. You'll be wonderful parents." His voice was husky with emotion. Jessa had stepped up as well, wrapping her arms around Zari and squeezing gently. "I love you guys. I'm so happy for you! Once I get back home, I'm going to get started on a baby blanket for the little pumpkin." Turning, Jessa threw her arm around Emmett's back and leaned in toward his shoulder. Being so close to him, smelling him, touching him, caused a physical ache in her gut. She'd known she could never have him, and Jessa would never have wanted to break up her friend's marriage. She couldn't help but feel attracted to him, to love him in a way she knew wasn't quite right. Hearing they were pregnant tore her soul in two. She wanted this for Zari, she wanted her best friend to be happy and knew she'd be a fantastic mother.

The darker part of her felt a sucker punch, knowing this sealed the deal. He would never leave her. Emmett was far too good a man to split up a family, and the coming baby all but guaranteed any hope of being with Emmett was long gone. Thing was, a big part of her attraction to him was his fierce display of faithfulness to his wife. In all honestly, what she wanted was for this good man to choose her over his wife, which would mean he wasn't as good and faithful as she believed him to be, which would definitely lessen her attraction for him. Even as she had these thoughts, she hated herself for them. Tears smarted her eyes again, but for a different reason this time. Jessa let them fall. She forced a smile to hide her pain.

Livvie stood there awkwardly, feeling oddly intimate with Zari after having straddled her still body and pressed Zari's quiet lips with her own, while attempting to resuscitate her. Emmett unnerved her. He was sexy as hell but married – she'd already made that mistake once and wasn't keen on getting into a mess like that again. Besides that, she'd seen his torn-up back and that told her one thing: the guy was broken. And broken as she was herself, she didn't need it compounded with the guilt of adultery and a guy carrying the baggage of physical abuse. Truly, she just wanted the roads cleared out and to see if the guys could get her car running so she could go home. If she still had one, that was. Silent, she pulled out a chair from the dining room table and sat with her back to everyone else, arranging Iris for a feeding. Livvie closed her eyes and listened to the conversation droning on behind her. All she'd wanted was shelter in the storm that night. She didn't want friends or the responsibility that came with them. She'd been trapped here for days and while grateful for the help these people had offered, she was really just plain over it all.

Catching up on the events of the last several days, there were tears and laughter as the sun set outside. Zari stood shakily, lighting a candle in the darkness and giving a wave as she headed up the stairs. Emmett was far too keyed up to sleep. "Guys, I'm going to walk her up and make sure she's settled down. I'll be back down in a minute." Mr. Grady and Maylie had set about the evening task of setting up candles throughout the living room and dining area. The oddity of the situation had worn off and spending days without electricity had become a new normal. Jessa watched Emmett walk up the stairs behind his wife, the sweet pain of longing heavy in her chest. She pressed her hand against her heart and rubbed, forcing cheer in her voice as she went to help the elderly couple light the room.

Their bedroom had been cleaned. Emmett stopped in the doorway, remembering the last time he'd been inside. The bed had been neatly remade, the vomit cleaned up off the floor. All his laundry had been picked up and placed in a basket. "Doing okay, babe?" He was thankful to be home but worried she'd stop breathing again, even though she was taking the new medicine. That had been some scary shit, and never in his life did he want to see it again. Zari melted into the bed and he pulled the quilt up over her. "Warm enough?" She smiled and patted the side of his face. The stubble along his jaw was thicker than she'd seen in it a good long time. "Tired," she whispered. "I know. I'll be back up to check on you in a bit. I'm just too wound up to rest right now." Emmett pulled the door only half shut as he left, just in case she needed him for something. Heading back down the stairs, he was struck by the beauty of the candlelit rooms, the flickering shadows on the walls. "Wow. I've never seen the house lit this way. It's lovely," he said as he hopped off the bottom step. "Thanks."

"Come on over here, Emmett. I want to tell you about something that happened while you were away." His voice was serious and Emmett's stomach churned. He was weary from different sorts of "news" he'd had thrown at him over the last few days. Regardless, he sat down on the couch next to Mr. Grady.

"What's going on?"

"Oh, nothing now. But the other night, during the storm. I took the girls back down to the basement, and we all went into your little utility room, you know? Anyway, somehow a whole mess of snakes had gotten in there and just covered the floor. I've been having trouble with snakes over to my place lately, but they've stayed outside, thankfully. But Emmett, there were *hundreds* of snakes in that room. I can't imagine how they got in there, but that little Jessa, she grabbed a bottle of bleach and threw it on 'em, and they burnt right up! You ever heard of anything like that? Couldn't believe it. The smell was something awful, let me tell you. Once the storm was over, I got your shovel out of the shed and went down with a garbage bag, scooped those fried up remains in and got them out of here. It was the strangest thing. But I wanted to let you know in case you had a crack in the foundation somewhere they were getting in. "

Involuntarily, Emmett shivered. He was glad Zari hadn't been here to see it. Her phobia would have had her going ballistic. "Thank you for taking care of that, James. Appreciate it. We'll have to take a looksee down there, see how they could've gotten in. I can't imagine…I wonder what sort of snake could react that way to bleach. I've never heard of that before. Crazy."

Mr. Grady had scooped the dead, burnt snakes up with the shovel. The work caused spasms in his old, arthritic back and joints but still he'd completed the task alone as he'd been raised in a generation that taught him dirty work was done by the men and women needed to be protected from it.

After he was finished, he'd gotten down on his hands and knees and scrubbed the floor until it sparkled, satisfied he'd cleared out any lingering residue of the encounter.

Mr. Grady had indeed cleaned up most of the snakes and removed them from the house.

Most.

But not all.

Because not all of them were dead.

Chapter Nine

Vomiting Fatigue.

"When the sun has set, no candle can replace it."
— George R.R. Martin

It was strangely quiet in the house now that their guests had gone home. Ten days had passed since Emmett and Zari had returned from the hospital, and Livvie and Iris, Jessa, and James and Maylie had remained for a few days after that until the power had come back on, and they'd gotten Livvie's car running again. Jessa was not quite so lucky – her vehicle was destroyed beyond repair, but once the power was on and the phone lines open again, she'd been able to reach her insurance company. They covered the cost of a rental vehicle. Emmett had walked over to the Grady house to be certain it was structurally sound before he let the elderly couple leave for home. He'd found his truck at the county impound, but they'd waived half the fee due to the "act of God" that had caused him to abandon it. Life had settled back into an uneasy rhythm. Zari held a great burden she desperately needed to release, and Emmett worried over Zari, pestering her about taking her medication and rarely sleeping, instead staying awake to watch Zari as she slept and make sure she kept breathing. He was exhausted, but unable to keep his eyes shut for longer than short bits of time at night. His panic over what he had almost lost was far too great.

Zari lay awake, aware that Emmett was watching her and feigning sleep anyway. Over and over in her mind, she strung the words out that needed to be said, rearranging them in a way that might make sense to her husband. A difficult task when she could barely figure a way to get the situation to make sense to herself. Even as she thought them, she stuttered the words.

The alarm was ringing. Buzzing. Shoving a knife of noise through her groggy brain. Zari felt a bit of drool on the side of her mouth and dragged the back of her hand across it after slapping the alarm off. "Em. Emmett. Babe." She flopped her arm over to his side of the bed, expecting to collide with his warm body, but he wasn't there. He must already be awake. Pushing back the covers, she stood slowly. Dizziness still sometimes overcame her and she'd learned to move with caution. Shivering, she pulled the quilt off the bed and drew it around her shoulders, and headed downstairs. There he was, a cup of coffee in hand, wearing a wrinkled dress shirt and flannel pajama bottoms, staring through the back window at what was once their porch. The debris of it had been cleared away and he'd promised to rebuild it, but for now it simply sat—an empty void where something lovely once had been, the yard overgrown with weeds and tall grass and sticks that had fallen in the big wind. So much still needed to be done, but he'd been trying to take the days a little easier. He'd felt better since leaving the hospital and hadn't fainted again, but was constantly aware of the possibility. Between that, worry for Zari and the baby, pressure to get all the damage from the storm fixed, and work, Emmett was long past exhausted. Too exhausted to rest, too fatigued to hold still. Purple smudges beneath his eyes told the story of his sleepless nights and the ever-present ache and muscle pain in his back seemed worse by the day. Emmett arched, trying to work the kinks out of it. Life would settle down soon. He was sure of it. Right now, though, he had to get to work. The semester was already so behind since the storms had hit. Classes had been cancelled for several days – which had been good when he was in the hospital, but even after the university had re-opened and he'd returned to work, half his students had still been unable to attend class or even submit work online from home. So much still needed to be done before exams and the weight of it left his shoulders rounded forward as he leaned until his forehead connected with the cool glass of the window. He was going to be late if he didn't get moving, and though in his mind he rallied, his legs were too tired to motivate. Weariness was bone deep. Emmett pressed the coffee mug to his lips and tipped his head back, guzzling the remainder of the last hope for energy he possessed. Turning, he saw Zari on the stairs and he smiled. "You were sleeping so hard. I didn't want to wake you."

"I'm not the one I'm worried about. Are you sleeping at all?" Zari asked seriously. She finished her descent and walked toward him, wrapping her arms around him and squeezing. Zari leaned her head into his chest. "Have you eaten?"

"Not hungry."

"Babe. You've got to eat and you've got to sleep. You're going to end up sick again."

"I'm just having trouble getting back into a routine. Things will settle down soon, I'm sure. I have this nagging feeling something bad is about to happen." He shrugged. "I don't know. A little anxiety is normal after what we've been through, I guess."

"Maybe you should go back to the doctor. I'm sure they could give you something to help you sleep."

"No! No. I don't want to be drugged. I need to be awake, in case you—"

"Sweetheart, I'm taking the new medicine and the doctor said I should be fine now. You can't stop sleeping forever."

"I need time, Zari. You don't understand how terrifying it was to see you like that. Don't you know that you are everything to me? *Everything.* The family I needed when I was growing up, the family I wished I had, someone to swoop in and save me from that hell, all of that is what you are to me. You're my whole world. I can't make it without you. I love you so much." He'd set the coffee cup on the end table and held her against him, his cheek pressed against her head. "You are so precious to me. I can't breathe without you."

"And *you* are precious to *me*. I need you to be strong and healthy too, you know? *We* need you to be. Besides, both of us need to spend these next few months sleeping as much as we can, right? Because once the little bugger gets here, it'll be a long, long time before we get solid sleep again." Zari laughed but was thinking: *We have no idea what's coming. I know they will come back for me and fight for this baby. I need you strong so you can fight beside me in this battle you know nothing about.* "You're going to be late for work, Professor. Come on. I'll fix you something to eat quick and you need to get going."

"All right. I'm almost ready, just need to get my shoes on and grab those papers I was grading last night. I'm so far behind with this class, I don't know what I'm doing." Running his fingers through his hair, he sat down hard on the dining room chair next to his brown loafers.

Walking back in from the kitchen, Zari held a sack lunch, a bottled water and a muffin in her hands. "Look, we have one blueberry muffin left and it's got your name on it, babe. Here's your lunch. Your graded papers are on the living room coffee table."

Shoes on, Emmett stood to peck her on the cheek and take

the offered gifts. "Thanks. I'll grab those. See you later. Love you."

Giggling, Zari held a hand out to grab his arm. "Emmett. Stop. You're still wearing pajama pants." Her giggles dissolved into full out howls of laughter. "Imagine if you went to class like that!"

"Good God. I'm so tired. I can't even think straight." Emmett's smile was sheepish. "I should've left five minutes ago." Instead, he jogged back up to their bedroom to quickly change. Properly attired, he dashed back through the living room, grabbing his keys and papers on the way out.

"Emmett," Zari whispered as she watched his truck back out of the drive, "when you get home, we need to talk."

~***~

Every day she was going to tell him.

Every day, she didn't.

Weeks had passed and Emmett had finally begun to sleep at night, at least a couple of broken hours. She watched him in the darkness, her heart tender and her stomach sick. Unsure if the uneasiness in her gut was actual illness or simply fear, Zari held one hand over her stomach and tried to think calming thoughts. *Emmett. My baby. Purple quilt squares. Sunshine streaming through branches in a forest. Quiet, rolling waves.* It wasn't working and suddenly the quiet boiling that had been present for over an hour exploded into a volcano that began to erupt before Zari could make it out of the bed. Lurching up while shoving the blankets out of the way, she stumbled as she ran for the bathroom with her hand over her mouth. Even as she ran, she felt the contents of her stomach bubbling up into her throat, bursting forth through her fingers and the coolness of the floor seemed distinctly incongruent when weighed against the hot fluid jostling for attention in her mouth. Finally, she slammed into the bathroom door, jiggling and turning the knob frantically with her free hand. Vomit had trickled past her hand and down the oversized T-shirt she'd slept in, sticking to her with great, sloppy circles. By the time she stood over the toilet, the rush of hot, vile liquid shot from her mouth as if it were a living thing and her only recourse was to crouch, balancing her body with her arms splayed out, one hand holding the corner of the cabinet and the other clutched around the toilet paper holder. Heavy dreads dangled on either side of her face and she wished she had the time or the strength or an extra hand to move them away. Sounds were coming out of her that she wanted to stop: gasping, wheezing, inexplicable roaring sounds that reverberated in her ears. Her chest was heaving with burning pressure and she ached to cry out for help but the constant rush of vomit up her throat strangled any screams. Tight cords stood out along each side of her neck, straining against her skin. Sweat had broken out across her forehead and Zari wondered how much more there could possibly be inside her, waiting to come up. The light flicked on and Emmett was there, wetting a washcloth to wipe her face and pulling her dreads back with his other hand. "Sweetheart, you're sick! You're…what is this? What did you eat?" The eyes she'd been squeezing shut for the duration of the misery opened and in the light she saw it: the thick black ooze that had sprayed over the seat and sides of the toilet, her arms and the front of her shirt. In horror, Zari watched as another agonizing fountain burst forth, filling the already near overflowing toilet up to the brim. Emmett rubbed circles on her back between her shoulder blades and the comforting action seemed at war with the raging storm within her. She'd taken to gulping fast chunks of air between the episodes of heaving, preparing for the next round as if she was going to be dunked underwater by some unseen hand. Finally it ended, the violent force disintegrating bit by bit until she lay on the floor crying, a black tar-like substance smeared across her face, staining her teeth with its filth. The smell of it was atrocious, foul and acrid like rancid meat. Zari realized with no little amount of embarrassment that she'd pissed her underwear. "This isn't right, Zari. It's so black, it could be blood. We'll have to call the hematologist in the morning, see if she can work you in. I don't want to take any chances. First though, let's get you into the shower. Can you stand, babe? Do you need me to help?" Zari sought the strength necessary to shake her head, but came up empty. Instead, she broke into a fresh round of sobs. "Here, I've got you." Gently, he scooped her up off the floor and pulled her soiled clothes from her weakened body. Reaching into the shower, Emmett turned the knobs and hot water shot from the head. He didn't stop to remove his own flannel pants as he lifted his wife into the shower and climbed in with her, holding her up. As he wiped the sticky residue from her face and arms, Emmett murmured softly to his wife. "Ssshhh, it's okay. It's okay. Everything's going to be all right."

Unable to respond, Zari leaned into his strength and simply allowed his strong arms to care for her as her mind jumped from thoughts of a desperate desire for sleep to ways to fight her family and Slither. Emmett had turned off the water and stepped out of the shower to grab a towel, keeping one hand on Zari's back as he did so. Wrapping her in it, he lifted her as if she weighed but an ounce and carried her back to their bed. His pajama bottoms were sopping wet and sticking to him in some places, sagging in others. He peeled them off and grabbed a pair of basketball shorts from his dresser, sliding them on. "I'm going to go clean the bathroom up. Try to get some sleep, babe." Her body limp and feeling as if she was made of rubber, Zari closed her eyes and drifted off. Emmett stood in the bathroom, disgusted and wishing he didn't have to clean the mess, but resigned to his duty nonetheless. Armed with paper towels, dish soap and bleach, he set to his task. The viscous black fluid and its putrid odor made him queasy and twice he was afraid his own stomach would begin to lurch, but eventually it was finished. As Emmett crawled back into bed with Zari, dawn was beginning and faint rays of morning light were creaking through the window. He placed his hand over her belly, pleased and proud and excited and terrified by the soft swelling that announced the presence of their child. Emmett glanced up at the clock. One more hour until he had to get up for work. Nestling his head down on the pillow, he spent that hour worrying.

~***~

"Did you call the doctor?" Emmett had called after his first class had trudged out the door, twenty-seven young people and one sixty-ish, silver-haired man who had spent the last two hours staring at him as if they'd rather be in prison getting a homemade gang tattoo than be there in his classroom, listening to him prattle on about Munro and Kerouac.

"Yes. They can see me at two o'clock today. Can you come?"

"I'll meet you there. If I can't find someone to cover my class, I'll just cancel it. I want to hear what she has to say. How are you feeling?"

"Better. I drank a little tea this morning and it stayed down. I'm kind of still afraid to eat, though."

"Will you be okay to drive?"

"Yeah. I'm all right. I'll see you at the doctor's office, okay?"

"Love you."

"Love you too, babe."

Zari hung up the phone and crawled back into her spot on the couch, dragging a quilt up over her as she went. *I'm not sure what the doctor might say about this, but I'm almost positive this was another manifestation of Slither. They're messing with me, trying to prove they can still control me and my body. Bullshit. They can't have me. I will fight this until I die.* There was no more putting it off. Who knew what else her family or that effing snake would do to her? Emmett had to know so he could stand beside her and fight. Or – and she couldn't deny this possibility – leave her. Either way. She had to tell him.

~***~

Sitting in the frigid waiting room, Zari bounced her legs alternately as a way to ward off the cold and her anxiety. She flipped through an outdated magazine without really reading any words, checked the time, checked the door. He should be – oh, she saw his shadow approaching the glass door and smiled a few seconds later when he ambled in.

"Zari Delaney?" She stood when the receptionist with the frizzy orange hair and pink bifocals called her name. She met Emmett in the middle of the waiting room. Together, they followed the nurse back into a hallway with several doors on either side. They stopped at the third on the left and entered. "Doctor should be with you shortly," said the nurse, and softly closed the door.

"Still feeling ok—" Emmett's question was cut off when the

door blew open, and a miniscule blond woman in a white lab coat and a clipboard in hand – and who resembled nothing so much as a very somber elf – stomped in. Leaning in and shaking first Zari's then Emmett's hands with a strength that belied her size, she sat down hard on her little three-legged, wheeled stool and got straight down to business. Holding the chart aloft, Dr. Lance put on the black horn-rimmed glasses that had been resting on her chest attached to a green beaded chain and began spouting facts: "Zari Delaney, age twenty-seven, primigravida, seventeen weeks gestation, high risk with long QT syndrome and von Willebrand disease, type one. Anything I'm missing?"

Startled at the oddity of hearing these personal bits of her life stated with such detachment, Zari took a few seconds to answer. "Ah, no. That sounds about right."

"And what brings you in today?"

"I think I was vomiting blood last night. Or, rather, early this morning. It was black and…and…well, disgusting."

"Black? I don't suppose you brought in a sample for me, did you?"

Instantly feeling like an errant kindergartener, Emmett spoke up. "I didn't even think of that. I just cleaned the mess to get rid of it all."

"Most people do. All right, let's get you up on the exam table so I can take a looksee, Mrs. Delaney."

Dr. Lance busied herself by pulling a small wooden stool out from behind the door and standing on it in order to reach Zari and examine her. A small pen with a light blazed into Zari's eyes, then her ears, up her nose. A tongue depressor flattened her tongue as the physician checked her throat. Small, rough hands palpated her neck and the doctor said more to herself than anyone else, "I don't feel any nodes cooking." Zari blinked a bit at the sudden invasion of what felt like her entire body, but complied when asked to lie back on the table. Up her shirt went, and the doctor was pressing down in different places with her hands and then placing a chilly metal stethoscope to Zari's abdomen, listening. Dr. Lance was an excellent physician, well-regarded in her field, but nobody who knew her could accuse her of being gentle. Intelligent, brusque, and with a no nonsense attitude, what she lacked in social skills she more than made up for in ability. "Okay, this is what we're going to do." She held Zari's hand and pulled the much taller and bigger woman up to a sitting position. "I'm not seeing anything today that indicates bleeding, but with the baby to be concerned about, let's err on the safe side. I'm going to order some more bloodwork for you, and I want you to stop and get that done on your way out – second floor, fourth door on the right. If that shows your levels are declining, we'll up the amount of von Willebrand factor you're taking. All right?" Helpless to do anything other than nod, Zari and Emmett sat and watched as the tiny woman slammed the door in their faces.

"She didn't seem overly worried. I guess that's good." Emmett stood and handed Zari her peace sign purse, and Zari pulled her long, multicolored sweater over her T-shirt and peasant skirt. Fall seemed to be coming abruptly to their town and she was beginning to feel a chill no matter where she was. They stopped at the front desk to make a follow-up appointment and took the elevator down to the second floor, quickly finding the sign for the phlebotomy lab and stepping inside. Looking over her order sheet, the tall male lab tech offered to leach her body of some life-giving fluid in a flash. "Step into my lair," he laughed with a terrible accent that was intended to come across as Dracula. Emmett barked a laugh and immediately covered his mouth with his hand. Zari rolled her eyes and plopped in the seat, slipping her arm free of her sweater. She winced as the tourniquet squeezed her flesh and the tech pressed the inside of her elbow with an expert hand. "Ah, yes. Nice and plump, I've got it right here," he said as a fat blue line appeared beneath her skin. The alcohol swab was quick and cold, followed by the small needle that slid easily into the vein. Zari watched, unblinking, as the vial filled with blood. Two vials. Three. "That's it," announced the vampire. "If you feel dizzy or shaky there are crackers on the table just over there." He pointed to a small table littered with packets of buttery disks. Grabbing one, Emmett handed it to Zari, who tossed it into her purse. As they walked back out to the parking structure, he looped his arm around her waist and pulled her close, tipping her face up for him to kiss her. "I love you. I'll see you at home." Zari clicked her key fob to unlock her car door and slid in, immediately locking the doors once inside. She started the car then sat for a moment, munching on her crackers. Emmett had taken off purposefully in one direction, changed his mind and headed the other way. After ten minutes, he grabbed his key fob from his pocket and clicked the alarm. Following the irritating beeping sound, he finally located his truck and started for home.

Of course Zari made it home before he did. Emmett pulled into the drive, and turned off the truck. Grabbing the bag of takeout he'd stopped on the way home for, he headed in and found Zari asleep on the couch, Raya Yarbrough's lovely voice belting from Zari's phone. "Sweetheart, I stopped and got us something to eat. Wake up, sleepyhead. Can you try to eat something?" Suddenly ravenous, Zari sat up in an instant.

"What'd you get?" She reached for the container of food eagerly.

"Well, I got two cheeseburgers and a fry. You get a tossed salad and a fry. And I picked you up a sweet tea."

"Thanks, babe. All of a sudden I am so hungry." Unsnapping the lid to her salad, Zari dumped dressing over the top and grabbed her plastic fork from the bag. Intent on filling her growling belly, Zari shoved forkful after forkful into her mouth, barely stopping to chew. Emmett watched her as he downed his burgers, laughing at the obvious intensity of her hunger. It made him happy, seeing this effect of her pregnancy. It was good to see something so normal going on with her. His eyes sparkled as he watched her chowing down. The last piece of lettuce had been devoured, and finally Zari looked up to see Emmett watching her. The look on his face was sweet and for a moment it hurt her, knowing she was about to take that away from him. "Emmett. Come here. I want to tell you something."

Terrified but resolved, Zari took a deep breath and held Emmett's hand in her own. "I want to talk to you about my family."

Concerned, Emmett's eyes softened. "Babe, *we* are our own family. You don't have to talk about the way they hurt you. I know it's hard on you. That's the past. What matters is now."

"No, Emmett. I need to talk about this. And I need you to listen. What I'm about to tell you is, well, it may sound unbelievable, but I want you to keep in mind that I have never lied to you. I wouldn't lie to you. Do you trust me?" She stared intently at his face, her gray-green eyes locked on his oceans of blue.

"What's this? Zari, of course I trust you."

Zari took a long sip of sweet tea, then resumed holding her

husband's strong hands. She looked directly into his eyes. "There are things in this world that people don't understand. Supernatural beings and entities and even other realities."

Emmett watched his wife intently. This didn't sound like Zari at all, and he was more than a little confused about where the conversation was going. Zari pushed forward, spilling the facts she'd known since childhood.

"Generations ago, my great-great-grandparents became involved with a sect of people who pledged fealty to a serpentine entity known as Slither. Allegiance with the serpent meant promising not only their lives, but that of their future lineage as well, to servitude. Through the ritual necessary to become part of Slither, the snake would enter their bodies through the mouth, only leaving once its mission had been achieved: to lay an egg within the individual that would eventually become a living snake within the person, surviving only to feed from others, which in turn fed the master snake, Slither." This part Zari had spat out almost robotically, desiring to get the explanation out as fast as possible. Emmett's face was nothing if not perplexed, and she squeezed his hands tighter in an unconscious effort to hasten his understanding. "Slither must always be fed. It's how it gets stronger. During a feeding, the snake will rise up from the gullet of the servant and into the mouth of the one being fed from, forcing itself down until it can feed from the person's insides, and must continue until Slither is sated. Are you understanding me, Emmett?"

He rose from the couch quickly, running his trembling hands through his curly brown hair as he paced. "I… I can't quite grasp this, Zari. It isn't making sense to me. This cannot be real."

"Why would I lie to you, Emmett? "

"I don't think you're lying, but you're not thinking straight, you've been ill and the medicine, maybe..." He threw his hands out to the sides, pleading. "You can't expect me to just *believe* you." Exasperated, he lifted his eyes to look at her.

"I'm not crazy." Zari jumped up, pounding herself on the chest as her voice rose. "Do you think I *want* this? I don't! I've been trying to get away from it my entire life!" Zari choked a sob as it bubbled up her throat. Her throaty voice rose to a higher, shakier pitch. "I never wanted to tell you this, but I have to now because we are in danger!"

"Danger? What do you mean by that?" Emmett stopped pacing and stood in front of her, his hands on her shoulders. "Zari! What do you mean, you're in danger?"

"Not just me, Emmett. You, and the baby, too. Slither is coming for us."

In an instant, Emmett had changed. Back straight, chin up, dark blue eyes blazing. Whether Zari's words made sense to him or not, he understood that his family was being threatened, and his guard was up against the unseen threat. *Tap tap tap* went his fingers against his thumb, slowly. "Tell me how to stop this. Nobody is going to touch you." A snake god? No, his rational mind couldn't quite process that. But she believed her family was out to harm her and he knew for a fact they'd abused her before. Perhaps...well, perhaps her mind was imagining something. Trying to compensate for reality. Regardless, nobody was going to threaten his wife.

"Just listen. You need to fully understand this." Already exhausted from the conversation that was nowhere near ending, she sat back on the couch. Her voice was quiet, but firm. Emmett sat on the opposite end, then reached out and drew her to him so her back was against his chest and his arms solidly around her. "Know this, and don't doubt me: I have never fed. When I was old enough, and they tried to force me, I ran away. Remember that, Emmett. I don't want you to think I am like them, because I'm not. But when I was a child, I was made to watch them do it. The first time, I saw my mother feed from my grandmother. I walked in on it accidentally and it terrified me. Sometimes...sometimes during an illness, Slither allows two of its kind to feed from one another for strength, and my mother was sick from her pregnancy with Gianna. That's the kind of memory that still causes me nightmares. After, I was forced to watch them as they lured in drifters, runaways...these people, these *real people*, Emmett, and they'd invite them in, feed them dinner, and somehow trick them into going out back to the shed. Then they'd tie them down on a pallet and the snakes would come up out of their mouths and into the person. At first, always, the stranger would fight and thrash and try to scream but once the snake was down their throat, their voice would be cut off." She remembered with horrible clarity the sight of her father wiping blood from his mouth after a feeding. Zari's voice trembled and caught and she blinked hard against the memory. *It's over; I'm here, I'm home. I'm home.* "Blood would come running out of their mouths and noses and sometimes their eyes, drizzling down while the serpent fed and when the body was limp and its heart had stopped, the slimy snake would snap back into the mouth of my mother or grandmother or father. I was horrified, but threatened with my life if I didn't watch. The bodies would stack up, and every couple of weeks my father would go out back during the night and dig holes to dump them into. Our house was pretty isolated, which I guess was for a purpose, so nobody noticed the smell of the rotting bodies." She stopped to look back and see if Emmett was following her words. His eyes were squinted into narrow slits, his cheeks flushed, mouth set in a grim line. He was trying to understand, she could tell. "Look, babe. I know this is hard to believe. I know that. But it's true."

"I'm…I'm trying. It may take some time for this to sink in. I'm not sure, exactly. But keep going. I need to know what the threat is so I can protect you." There was a threat against his family, and that was all that mattered to Emmett. He zeroed down on that one thought, focusing.

Zari took another long sip of sweet tea then settled back into the safety of Emmett's arms. He hadn't left yet, and that was encouraging. Her heart thumped somewhat erratically in her chest. She remembered suddenly the doctor's words about not becoming overly stressed and smiled mirthlessly. "There comes a time in the life of each follower when allegiance is demanded. Gianna was young when she pledged and promised her life to Slither. I refused and was beaten multiple times. My grandmother…well, let's say she can be intimidating. But I would not cave in, no matter what she hit me with. My mother, she's weak. And mean. She never hit me but she watched while Nan did and she never lifted a finger to stop it. And I told you before that I left home at seventeen. That's the truth. I ran away in the middle of the night with just a backpack of clothes, hitchhiked for awhile. Anything just to get away from them. And you know I lived on the streets for a few months. That was hard and scary but I'd do it again in a heartbeat. But I made it out, or so I thought. I hadn't heard anything in all these years. I met you, and we've been so happy. Emmett, I swear to you that I wouldn't have brought this on you if I thought they would come after me. I thought I had escaped, I thought…I thought it was over. I just wanted to be normal, and be with you and have this life we'd built. And then the nightmares got worse, and the shaking started in my hands. I didn't want to believe they were coming for me again."

"I don't understand…well, any of this. But how are the tremors related to your family or this…ah, snake?"

"That's the thing, Emmett. Slither can control just about anything. That day I ran home from the market, it was there. This little girl came at me, and told me Slither was coming for us. That's why I ran home – I was afraid it had somehow come here and hurt you. And I think Slither caused the storms. But the night I stopped breathing, I was dreaming about Nan attacking me and she was wrapping this film over my face and I couldn't breathe. And the snake was just…everywhere. And I woke up back at my parent's place, tied on a pallet."

"No. That's not right, Zari. I know exactly where you were, and you were in a hospital bed not moving at all. Are you sure this isn't just a nightmare that feels real to you?" Relief washed over him. This wasn't real, after all. Just a terrible, realistic dream she'd had. Emmett closed his eyes for a second and cleared his throat.

"Believe me, Emmett. I wish it was. But they told me that I was in another reality. I didn't believe it at first, but then I could hear you talking to me, telling me to wake up and they said I was in a coma at the hospital. I still don't really understand how that was possible, but it happened. I tried to fight. I fought the straps on my arms until my skin was a bloody mess and Nan slapped me across the face so hard she knocked me out." Emmett remembered the way the bruises had simply appeared on Zari as they'd watched, and how strange it had been that the bruises on her wrists had been identical. Zari's words had picked up pace, as if they were tumbling down a hill, gaining speed as they went, head over heels. "And they said they were going to hurt you if I didn't accept Slither and promise, and I refused so they said they'd kill us both. I spit in Nan's face and I tried to get my mother to help me, but she's too cowed by my Nan and father to make a move they don't approve of. I'd rather die than than feed off innocent people. That's repulsive." She shuddered even as she said it. "But then they said they'd let me – let *us* – go if I gave them the baby."

"*WHAT?*" Emmett's tone was ferocious. He gripped Zari's shoulders painfully hard. "No!"

"I said no! I didn't even know about the baby until they told me, and I said I wouldn't do it. They were furious with me and threatened you again. *They* were the ones who caused you to get sick. They did something to screw with your heart. And I begged them to stop and they said I had to choose, and… I don't really….well, I'm not sure what happened next. Nan hit me. I blacked out and woke up back in the hospital with you. At first I thought they had let me go because I wasn't cooperating, but I don't think they will let me out of this. I think me getting sick last night was another way to toy with me, just to let me know they still have control over my body. I know it in my heart, Emmett, they are going to come for this baby. They want to raise it in my place, make our child a servant of Slither. They aren't going to stop until they get their hands on our baby."

"Like hell they will," Emmett growled. The sides of his jaw twitched, anger darkened his blue eyes. Sharply, he inhaled through his nose. "They won't touch you. I'll kill them all."

"I don't know how to fight them. I'm scared, Emmett." Her voice trembled.

"Zari, look. I'm not going to pretend I understand everything you've told me, but nobody is going to threaten my family. You are *mine*. The nights I spent crying as a little boy because my mother wouldn't protect me from that monster...well." His jaw worked, twitching, and his eyes narrowed to slits. "No child of mine will suffer that way. I promise you that. Look at me." Zari sat up, wiping at tears as she did so. Her body ached for sleep or food or sex, she couldn't tell for sure. She wanted something that filled her up completely and left her feeling safe. "I will not let this happen. I would give my life to protect the two of you, but first I will kill any bastard that even thinks of laying a hand on you, and that's a promise you can count on."

"I was so afraid to tell you, Emmett. I was afraid you would leave me." Relief sparked through her, an electrical current of gratitude.

"I will never leave you. *Never.* I love you."

"I love you, too."

"We'll get through this, come hell or high water. I will keep you safe at any cost. Believe me, Zari."

And she did.

~***~

There had been part of Zari – a much bigger part than she'd realized – that had been ready to accept that Emmett would leave once he learned the truth. Even as she'd spit the words out almost robotically, she'd watched him, waiting for his tone to become distant or his body language to pull away from her, creating a chasm too wide to be bridged. Still, she'd plowed on, telling him, finally releasing the secret that had been buried deep within her for so long, and through her fear, the relief of it was unexpectedly startling. When Emmett had drawn her to him, wrapping her safely in his arms and sworn to protect her rather than leave her, a stubborn, angrily independent piece of her spirit that had burrowed down to the very center of her being, broke free. There was no longer a wedge between them. No longer would she have to watch her words, her truth as she spoke to him. At once, this knowledge was both freeing and paralyzing. He knew all of her now, every last miserable, ugly bit. Any illusions he'd had regarding his wife had been ripped away. And still – and still, he strengthened his hold on her, drawing her in to him, loving her. Zari turned to him then, the love she had always felt for the man she'd married increased tenfold, binding her spirit to him in a way she could not understand. It was a searing, raw pain inside her, leaving her both agonized and insatiably hungry for him.

She'd been laid bare before him, the shame and darkness within her as unwillingly displayed as the pink and white lines that scarred her husband's back.

He still wanted her. And that left her wanting him.

Roughly, she kissed him, her own lips feeling hot and swollen with desire. His mouth, surprised at first, then softly yielding to hers as she slipped her tongue inside, enjoying the heat of his breath. Emmett tugged her shirt over her head and she raised her arms to let him. As her shirt drifted to the floor, she worked to release him from his own. In moments, there was nothing between them any longer: no secrets, no pain, no fabric. Just the two of them, hot skin against hot skin: pressing, arching, seeking. Loving. A slight startle as their bodies joined; a brief pause as they settled into their union, rocking rhythmically, hip to hip. Without thought, they were bridging a gap they'd not realized existed between them. Blindly, Zari dug her nails into his back, clawing, drawing him closer. Emmett wrapped his arms around her back, clutching her to him just a little too tightly. She gasped, trying to catch her breath despite his clenching grip and he squeezed even harder. They tumbled to the cool hardwood floor, briefly slamming into the coffee table – the corner of which bruised Zari's hip -- before Emmett reached out and gruffly shoved it onto its side, away from their twisting bodies. Each of them breathless and somewhat panicked at the knowledge they could not physically climb within the other, as they each desperately wanted to do. Flipping again, Emmett growled into her ear, "You are *mine!*" as he reached up and released her dreads from their tie, the heavy, somewhat scratchy feel of them hitting his skin with a jolt of pleasure that only added to the mounting desire that had nearly hit an unbearable level. "Emmett!" she cried his name as she arched one last time against him and he held tight to her, burying his face in her neck, her hair draped around him like a curtain as he sucked softly on her neck and filled her.

~***~

"You should have told me." They'd held each other for hours on the floor, but had eventually climbed back up on the couch. Emmett lay on his back and Zari lay against him, belly to belly. She'd dragged a quilt up over their bodies, and curled into his bigger, stronger frame, enjoying the way his strength made her feel small and loved. His finger traced her jaw, neck, and breast and she breathed out heavily, scrambling for a reason that made sense. *I didn't tell him before because…why? I didn't think he would believe me? I didn't want to burden him. Is that it? No, Zari. Tell him the truth.*

Her voice was soft, fragile. She whispered, "I was afraid."

Emmett matched her tone. "Afraid of what? Me?" He sounded somewhat insulted.

"Yes." There it was, then. Underlying her desperate love for this man there had always been a thin layer of fear: physically, he could overtake her if he decided to. And she would have been helpless again, just like she had been as a child in the shed, watching her family murder people.

"Did you think," he paused, gulped, went on, "that I would hurt you?"

"No. Yes. Maybe." Barely a whisper; he had to struggle to hear her words.

"Zari. I love you. I would *never* hurt you." He said this with conviction. He held onto her body, biceps flexing.

"You might, but not on purpose."

Emmett lay still, thinking. They were still whispering in the darkness. He pulled the blanket up closer around her shoulders. "Do you really think that of me? Do you think I would harm you? Hit you?"

"I've always been afraid." Of everything. Everyone.

"What…what have I done to make you think that about me?" He felt lost, inadequate, somehow monsterish. Had his own demons made him so frightening to her and how could he have been unaware of it?

Her voice was slightly muffled, buried against the hair on his chest. "N-nothing. I don't know." Briefly, she shrugged. "They said they loved me. When I was small. But they…beat me. Over and over." Zari flinched, as if remembering the strikes. Emmett wrapped his arm securely around her. Imagining her family hitting her, bruising her flesh, making her cry – he ground his teeth. With his opposite hand, he reached up into her hair, clutching a fistful of it for a moment, then released it and held her head closer to the center of his chest. Zari listened to the beats of his heart, his breaths in and out, and worked to match her own heartbeat, her own breaths to his. Hot tears stung her eyes. Drops of salty water sat fat and helpless on her eyelashes. Had she looked up she would have seen matching wetness in Emmett's blue eyes. His spilled over and ran down his face, waterfalls of emotion he was unable to stop.

"Babe, I'm so sorry they hurt you. I'm *so* sorry. I understand what it's like to have someone you trust…hurt you that way. And I, I *hate* that you know what it is to be beaten that way, that they took your innocence away from you. I'd give anything…I'd let him burn my back again," Zari didn't have to ask who '*him*' was, "if I could just take this pain away from you. I think surviving that kind of childhood, it breaks something inside us. But honey, you can believe me when I say that there is *nothing* you could do that would induce me to hurt you. I couldn't. I couldn't do it. I love you so much. You are part of me. Listen, I could not harm you. I could not leave you." He tipped her chin up, so she was forced to see him. Zari squeezed her eyes shut. "Look at me. *Look at me.*" His voice was demanding. She could not refuse him. Pools of gray-green stared at him, unblinking. "You are my entire soul. I cannot live without you. I will not ever raise my hand to you. Do you understand me?"

Zari sniffed, wishing she could melt into the blanket and disappear. "I'm sorry."

"Stop apologizing! You've not done anything to be sorry for!" Visibly, she flinched again. He gentled his tone. "You never need to be afraid of me."

"I love you. I'm just…I'm messed up, Emmett. And I didn't want you to know," she said the words and hated them. Her voice was thick with misery.

"Loving you means loving every part of you. Listen. When we first met, I was afraid," he coughed, "for you to see my back. It took me a long time before I could let you. Sometimes, I would think of letting you see me and just the thought of it would break me out in a sweat. But I knew you loved me and I started to trust you. And there came a time when I decided if I was going to love you, and we were going to build a life together, you would have to know. I couldn't continue to hide it, though I wished I could. These marks, they're my shame, forever. Showing them to you nearly broke me. Do you know that? I waited, that night, after I let you take my shirt off – that first night I ever took you to bed. Remember? I was eaten up with desire for you, with feelings I'd never had for anyone before. I knew I couldn't keep putting it off. And I wanted you so much, I couldn't stand it." His jaw was resting on her forehead as he spoke, and she felt the hard bone of it twitching against her. The hand that sat so sturdily on her shoulder clenched in a fist, then released: clench, release, clench, release. "I wanted, needed, to touch all of you, and I wanted you to know all of me. But I was so damned afraid. Scared to death that you would see me and be disgusted by the sight of it. That you would leave and I'd never…well. But you didn't leave, did you? No. You looked at me, at all of it, and I stood there, bared before you, raw. Waiting for your rejection. Trembling. Holding my breath. I closed my eyes, and felt you come closer. I felt your hands, tracing the scars, your fingers light on my damaged skin. Eventually," Emmett swallowed hard, "I felt your hands on my shoulders, holding tight, and your m-mouth on my back, kissing the marks, sliding your tongue across them. For the first time, I felt desirable. As a man – a whole man. You didn't run. You welcomed me, you showed me that you wanted *me*. All of me. And I told you then, about what he'd done. I thought you might think me weak. But you didn't. You took me to bed, and let me love you and you, Zari, *you* made me a whole man." He took a ragged breath, drawing it deep inside him, rubbing his thumb across her cheek. "I know what it is to want to hold the broken pieces of you back. But Zari, I *want* those pieces of you. I want the dark, filthy parts you keep hidden. I want to claim all of you, every piece, every tiny crevice. I want all of you to be mine, just as you have claimed all of me. Don't be afraid, Zari. You cannot scare me away."

Zari was weeping in earnest now; great, ugly sobs that soaked the wiry hairs of his chest, leaving tiny rivers that traveled his skin, dripping past his nipples, down his sides. Mucus ran unceremoniously from her nose, unchecked, and occasional drool dribbled from her mouth. Harsh, racking sobs escaped her and she clutched him, bottled up fears from her childhood finally escaping after years in exile. She felt it then, the pain of the beatings, the leather of the strap her grandmother had whipped against her, the pummeled fists on her face, her stomach, her back as she lay on the floor of her childhood home. She felt, fully *felt* and acknowledged the horrors she been forced to witness as a young girl; the conflicting of feelings she held for her family: hate, disgust, disappointment…and still, love. Somehow. She couldn't understand it, and she wished she could dismiss the feeling, but it was there and nothing to do about it. It wasn't the people they had become, or perhaps always were, that she loved. She understood that now. But she grieved the family she thought she had. She mourned the loss of trust and innocence. And losing that bit of hardness inside of her, the solid piece of misery she'd held in the center of her being for so long, was frightening. She wept for the family she had lost, and she wept for the little girl she'd been. Emmett held her tight against him, murmuring soft and gentle words against her ear. "It's okay," he said, and "We'll be all right," and "You are my heart," and perhaps most important, "I love all of you. You've always belonged to me." At this, Zari wept even more frantically, pulling herself away from Emmett and then allowing him to draw her in close again; a bundle of exhausted, nervous energy.

She was suddenly filled with the bone chilling terror of knowing, truly *knowing*, that she was raw and exposed before this man, that he could see inside her and knew the worst, the darkest parts of her. Zari was so afraid her very skin hurt, the way it does during a bad bout of influenza, when it seems the lightest touch of a sheet or even air brushing against the flesh must leave it scabbed and raw. Wind roared in her ears to the beat of her heart, and when she was finally spent, when she no longer had the strength to weep or hiccup or sob, Emmett slid out from beneath her and scooped her up in his arms. He carried her to their bedroom, where he made love to her again. Tenderly, softly, making her believe his words and his love for her, the way she had for him so long ago, the night he first allowed her to see the marks on his back.

And he kissed her scars away.

~***~

He was so heavy.

Aaron, his mother's boyfriend, came in during the night. Emmett heard the soft turning of the doorknob, the creak of the door, the whisper of a bare foot on the carpet. He thought of the sword tucked safely under the bed. Could he reach it in time? Bile rose unbidden to his throat; strong and acidic on his tongue, it lapped at the back of his mouth, warm and insistent. He thought to reach beneath the bed and draw the sword up and under him, flinging it out at an opportune moment and hoping he hit something vital. Shuddering, he imagined the blade scoring flesh.

SLITHER

Could he do it? "Yes," he thought, he could. Tall and strong already at fourteen, he was confident he could take on his abuser. He thought to his arm, "Move", but the limb lay stiff and leaden along his side. "Move! Move! Move!" he screamed in his mind, but the arm seemed shrunken, somehow, wasted and unable to rouse itself.

Aaron was on him. Removing his pajamas, folding them and setting the clothes softly on the night stand. He would not cry out this time, he decided. No matter what happened. He wouldn't give the man the pleasure of his cries; he knew how much Aaron enjoyed the small sounds that sometimes ripped from his throat with the beat of the whip. A sensation like a swarm of buzzing bees filled his stomach and his heart beat erratically in his chest. He had failed again and hated himself for it. If only his arms would move! Instead, they lay stubbornly at his sides, useless as dead fish. The pain was coming now, whip after whip, and he felt his skin tearing open again, searing him to the bone with its awfulness. Despite his conviction, first a grunt, then a startled cry emerged from his mouth. Horrified, Emmett buried his face in the pillow. "Let me die," he prayed to anyone who might be listening. "If I can't fight, let me die to get away from him."

But Emmett did not die, and he could not force his arms to function. The sword remained in its hiding place, straight and helpless as Emmett himself. Aaron breathed out hard; a low, whooshing murmur of pleasure escaped his lips, and he collapsed forward against the bloody back of the boy in the bed.

Panicked now, Emmett gasped for air and once more strived to move his floppy lips; they'd gone frozen, pieces of plastic glued to his skin that couldn't possibly work the right way. He knew what would come next and his shoulders quivered, working forward to cave in around his chest and protect...something. Aaron grabbed Emmett's wrists and held them over his head, pinning the boy down. With his opposite hand, he lit the cigarette dangling from his tightly pressed lips and a hoarse sound, a combination of laugh and cough spilled out, causing the cigarette to shake slightly in its place. Emmett waited, counting the drags on the smoke, anticipating the searing, burning pain that would soon take him. Emmett's left shoulder twitched, up and down, and the slight motion caused Aaron to grin around his cigarette. "I know you don't understand. But you don't have the mind of an artist. You can't...see...the beauty we've created together. I can, though. And it's breathtaking."

One last drag on his smoke; a long, deliberate exhale, and his steady hand pinched the cigarette from his lips, lowering it cautiously its special place. There was always the chance Emmett would move at the last second, and ruin the masterpiece. He didn't, though; he lay perfectly still and quiet but for the tiny, soft sounds – like a small kitten – that escaped his lips now and again. Tendrils of scent wafted up toward Aaron's face, and he sniffed deeply, inhaling the smell and flavor of burning flesh. It was the memory of that sweet, acrid scent that filled him; the pleasure of it drove him nearly mad with the wanting of it. He dreamed of it, and would sometimes wake with Emmett's mother in his arms, and bury his face in her hair, smelling the faint residue of shampoo and wishing it was the scent of singeing flesh on her son's back, instead.

~***~

Emmett stood naked, arms wrapped around his chest, feeling oddly detached from the pain. It had come so often by then; almost as routine as a dental appointment. Aaron quickly ripped the soiled sheets from the bed and replaced them with clean ones, motioning for the boy to come forward and get in. Numb, Emmett propelled forward on wooden legs. The sheets were cool against his skin, and he held himself rigidly on his right side, blanket drawn up no further than his hips, staring unblinking in the darkness. Aaron climbed into the bed next to him, causing a dip beneath his weight in the center of the mattress. Emmett's back seemed to have a pulse of its own, throbbing an erratic rhythm different from the heartbeat that was pounding in his ears. Movement of any kind caused air to dig deep into the wounds, catching his breath with the sharpness of it. The numbness had begun to wear off; the pain now was deep and visceral.

Next time, Emmett thought, next time, I will kill him. With that thought, he relaxed as much as he was able into the warm, strong arms of his abuser, and let unconsciousness take him. As he drifted away into the comforting black sea of nothing, he tapped his first finger – twice– on his thumb, and followed suit with the rest of his fingers, down and back, down and back. Tap-tap, tap, tap, tap.

Sarah woke, confused, reaching for Aaron in their bed and finding him gone. She lay quiet for a few minutes, listening. That was it, then. She could hear him across the hall in Emmett's bedroom. He was grunting, an ugly, masculine sound that made her shiver. With great effort she stood, bending down slightly to click the lamp on. In her dresser, she rummaged through the top drawer and pulled out her little box. Trembling, she used her teeth to tighten the latex tourniquet around her upper arm and waited a second, clenching and unclenching her fist. Obedient, a fat vein rose to the surface, a wide line as blue as Emmett's eyes. The first bite of the needle stung. She pushed it slowly, deliberately. The warmth spread quickly throughout her body, making her light and unburdened. Dropping the needle and tourniquet back into her little box, she turned the lamp back off and smiled. The sounds across the hall heightened for a moment; quick, furious and loud, then settled to a droning murmur. She closed her eyes, and slept.

Zari felt him leave the bed sometime in the night. She felt the depression in the mattress from his body raise up with the loss of his weight, and she came half-awake in the darkness. She expected him to go out, to the bathroom, perhaps, or for a glass of water.

Instead, he stood still in the darkness at the foot of the bed, looking up at the wall behind the headboard. Zari waited several minutes, slowly coming to full wakefulness, and finally sat up in the bed, allowing the quilts to fall down around her. Her curving, naked form was accentuated in the shadow of moonlight. She spoke quietly. "Emmett? Is something wrong?" Still, he stood motionless, fixated on the wall. Zari abandoned the blankets altogether, crawling across the bed and half-rose on her knees, pressing her palms to his abdomen and feeling the slight shudder contained within. "Emmett? Sweetheart? What's happening?" His chest rose and fell quickly and his arms slid automatically around her shoulders. "Tell me." Emotion worked across his face: a little line furrowing between his eyebrows, his nose scrunching, jaw twitching.

"I saw him. In my dream. Aaron was here. He held me down, in the pillow. I couldn't breathe." Emmett's breaths came at first in tiny, hurried spurts and with effort eventually began to slow down.

"It's okay, though, babe. He's not here. It's just us. Just us." Emmett's grip around her shoulders tightened, drawing her head in to rest on his stomach and leaving her own swollen belly pressing against his thighs, but his eyes remained on the sword on the wall above their bed.

"I used to hold it, you know. The sword, I mean. When I was young…when…" His voice trailed off for a moment. "I would sit on my bed with it, feeling the cold steel, the weight of it, touching the blade with my fingers. Planning. Imagining what it would be like, you know, to kill him. To shove it straight through him the next time he came for me. I would think how…how freeing it would feel to slice through his skin, to watch him bleed. And die. I wanted it. I wanted to watch the life drain from his eyes and know I'd done it. I slept with the sword beneath my bed, dreaming of the day I would use it. But I never did."

"But Emmett, you were just a child, just a little boy."

"Not by the end of it. I was seventeen when he finally left. *Seventeen.* God, Zari. I was a man grown! I could have…I *should have.* But I was weak. I was afraid. I allowed him to hurt me. *I allowed it.*" His hands trembled on her shoulders. "I could have fought him. I could have killed him. Instead, I lay still in my bed and let him rip me apart." Zari slid from the bed and stood behind her husband, touching the scars that marked him, hills and valleys both smooth and rough beneath her fingers. How many times? She had often wondered this. How many times had his lower back been flayed, the tender flesh torn apart by the monster? Years. Years it had taken to do this. His back had healed and been ripped open innumerable times. His mother had known it, and had offered no help for her son. Zari's heartbeat quickened with anger and keeping one hand on Emmett's back, the other drifted down to rest on her belly.

"Emmett. You are not weak. I've never known anyone as strong as you. The strength you've shown in overcoming this abuse is part of what attracted me to you. Do you know that? Because that night, that first night, I saw you and it never crossed my mind to turn away or be disgusted. It pained me, Emmett, to know you'd been hurt. I was in love with you already. That you trusted me enough to see you that way only strengthened my feelings for you. I felt furious, helpless with rage at the injustice of it. I felt sick, because I knew what it was like to be abused and wished I could take that from you. But when I touched you, I thought the scars were beautiful, Emmett, because they were part of you and part of the man you'd become. Emmett, I already loved you before I knew, and after…I thought," Zari stopped and bit her lip, continued, "I thought, if you could survive this, and be the man you were, then I could overcome as well. Your strength made me want to hide inside you and let you care for me, taking away my own pain. And it made me want to be strong, like you. But Emmett, I saw nothing then or now that made me think you were weak. *You* were not the one who did wrong. *He* was a sick, sadistic monster. *He* was the weak one. Never you."

"I should have…"

"You did. You survived. You survived it, Emmett. We both did. That was then. What matters is now."

Zari could hear a small, squeaking sound as Emmett's jaw worked, grinding his teeth. "I'm not a child anymore. I'm not weak. I won't let them have you, Zari, or our child. I *will* protect you. Believe me."

"I do. I believe you, Emmett. I believe you."

As she pressed her body against his and tilted her head in to his shoulder, she felt his muscles tense and straighten, drawing his entire body taut as if readying himself for battle. Zari wrapped her arms around him in the darkness, feeling his heartbeat, his breath, his strength. Somewhere in her core she felt an odd, fluttering sensation like the buzzing, half-frightened feeling one feels in the gut when an elevator suddenly moves and the impression of simultaneously falling and rising wars within. Quietly, she gasped and stiffened. Emmett turned to her. "What's wrong?"

"Nothing I…I felt…" Zari searched her mind, looking for a name for what she was feeling.

"What, babe? You felt what?"

A synapse struck; was it...yes. It must be. "Emmett, I...I think I feel our baby moving."

Instantly, he relaxed against her. His hardened muscles melted as she held him. He dropped a hand to her belly, cupping the small swelling of flesh there. His voice lowered, filled with wonder. "Our baby?" he asked, then stated the same words again. "Our baby." Slowly, he smiled, the moonlight catching and reflecting on his teeth, the crooked eyetooth seemed somehow brighter than the rest. Emmett lowered himself steadily until he sat on the bed before her, his large, capable hands encircling her waist. He leaned his forehead against the top of the small mound and pressed his lips to the center of it. "Zari, I love you so much. I love you. I love you," he murmured to her stomach, repeating himself over and over. She draped her hands behind his head, enjoying the feel of his soft curls in her fingers. "I love *you*, Emmett. I love you with all that I have. All that I am."

"I will find a way to keep you safe. I'll find a way." Emmett wasn't talking to Zari any longer, but to the tiny person he'd not yet met, but loved more than his own life.

Chapter Ten

Unmasking.

"And when at last you find someone to whom you feel you can pour out your soul,
You stop in shock at the words you utter— they are so rusty, so ugly,
So meaningless and feeble from being kept in the small cramped dark inside you so long."
— Sylvia Plath, *The Unabridged Journals of Sylvia Plath*

Living with her secret had been horribly painful and anxiety-inducing. Having it out in the open, at least with Emmett, was a release so great it lifted the stain of nightmares Zari had been trapped in. Sleep came so much more easily to her now. Although she was afraid of her family and Slither, she trusted Emmett. But the revelation had changed her husband in ways she wasn't sure could ever be made right.

Briefly, and on very few occasions since she'd been with Emmett, she'd seen a side of him that left her cold and unsettled. Usually this side of him came out when someone saw his scars or for some reason he had to tell another about his horrendous experiences as a child. The way her husband spoke, the tilt of his head, his gait and mannerisms were so unlike the Emmett she had fallen in love with, he could have been another person entirely. It was a coping mechanism, she was certain, a way he had developed to escape the nightmare he had lived in. This 'other' Emmett was kind and good and loving, but also brusque, short-tempered, and arrogant. He seemed to have slipped into this personality permanently now and while Zari didn't fear him, she wanted her absentminded professor back. Emmett seemed now always on alert, always ready for attack. Zari mourned that she had been the cause of the change in the man she loved so much. The baby was growing, as was her size and the child was active now, twisting and tumbling within her, distinct elbows and feet taking turns pummeling her insides. Since upping the dose of von Willebrand factor, Zari hadn't experienced any more bruising or vomiting of blood. Though some level of fear had become a constant companion, her pregnancy seemed to be going well and she was becoming excited about the baby.

Today she was twenty-five weeks in and en route to meet Emmett at her ultrasound. Every time she went for a doctor appointment, Zari expected to be told something had gone horribly wrong, but was happily incorrect in this assumption. She measured exactly right. Her blood pressure and blood sugar had remained stable throughout, and she felt great. The terrible and constant fatigue that had assaulted her during the first trimester had finally waned, and she had begun quilting again. It felt good to have the energy to be working at her passion again, feeling the rush of a creative outlet. Zari turned into the physician's lot. *There's Emmett's truck. He's so excited. I can't wait to see him hold this baby. Ow! The way you've been kicking me lately, little one, I think it's a safe bet you're going to be as leggy as your parents.* As she stepped out of the car, Zari pulled her coat as near to zipping as it possibly could go, given her burgeoning belly. Emmett slid out of his truck and walked toward his wife, hands in the pockets of his wool coat. "Hey, beautiful." Zari laughed and kissed his cheek. Their hands slid together comfortably in the fashion of longtime lovers, an unconscious coupling of strength and spirit. "Are you ready for this?" Zari asked.

"I'm so ready, babe. I can't wait to see his face." Emmett's own face seemed happy and tender and young.

"*His* face? It could just as easily be a girl, you know."

"I know. I guess I always imagined having a son first. "

"If it's a girl, do you think you'd be disappointed?"

"What? No. I'm just excited to meet our baby. What about you, though? Boy or girl?"

"I don't care. I'm happy. You know, I never thought I would have kids, because of…well, you know. Truthfully, I'm still so blown away at the thought of having my own baby, I'm still trying to grasp it. But I've thought of a few names I like for either gender."

"Yeah? We'll have to talk about that later. Here we are." Emmett opened the door to the office and ushered Zari in. He smiled brightly as the receptionist opened the side door in the office and said, "Come straight in. You're our first patient today." Settled in the tiny cubicle that was the ultrasound room, the nurse that had silently appeared seemingly out of nowhere handed Zari a paper dress, instructions about putting it on – leave the bra and underwear on, shirt and skirt off – and disappeared back to wherever she had come from. Seconds later, the sonographer came in. He was a forty-something-ish man with salt and pepper hair and large white teeth. "Ready to take a look at your baby? Lie back. I'm going to squeeze this gel on your belly and it's going to be cold." He talked fast and moved as he worked, pulling apart the modicum of modesty Zari had been clinging to as she held her paper dress closed. Nonplussed, the technician flicked the monitor on and grabbed up the wand to squish into the gel on Zari's abdomen, and started moving it in circles. "Mmmn. Mmmn hmmmn. Yes. All right. Heart, looks good. Brain, looks good. These are the new 3D images. Look, this is your baby's face." Emmett and Zari looked briefly at one another before glancing up to the screen, which held their gaze, mesmerized. Looking back at them was a round-faced, square-chinned little person. With a clarity so unbelievable it seemed almost wrong to view, they stared at their miracle on the screen. "Would you like to know the gender? Mr. and Mrs. Delaney, do you want to know if your baby is a boy or a girl?"

Emmett spoke first. "Zari, are you sure? Do you want to find out today?"

"I do. Do you still?"

"Yes."

Zari giggled. "Yes. Tell us!"

"You are about to be the proud parents of a little….drumroll please…dah dah dah dah! Girl. This is definitely a little girl."

"A girl? Are you sure?" Zari's heart soared in her chest, but she was worried Emmett might be disappointed. She chanced a peek at him anyway. Deep blue eyes sparkled back at her, a faint rosy tint darkening his cheeks. An easy grin spread across Emmett's face in a way that pulled at Zari's gut. It was so much the old Emmett, that smile. The mask was gone, at least in that moment and his shoulders relaxed and he stepped forward, squeezing into the ridiculously tight space between the wall and the table she lay on. "A girl, sweetheart. A daughter. I'm so happy!" Emmett bent down to plant a kiss on her lips, then snapped upright again, his questions directed at the sonographer. "She's okay, right? Our daughter is fine? She looks healthy?"

"As far as I can tell, she looks perfect. And in about fifteen more weeks, give or take a few days, you'll find out for yourself. Mrs. Delaney, there are paper towels to your left to clean the gel off with, and once you're dressed, you're free to go."

Emmett stuck his hand out to shake with the man. "Thank you, sir. I can't thank you enough."

"Don't thank me. You two are responsible for that new little person. I just get to shine a light on what's already done."

"Are you truly happy, Emmett?" she asked, suddenly shy.

"Absolutely. I couldn't possibly be happier. I had no idea how desperately I wanted a little girl until right this minute, and now there is nothing in the world I want more than to meet our daughter."

"I'm glad. I'm happy, too." A giddiness spread through her, followed by a sudden pang of reality. This was really happening. She smiled at her husband.

"What's the name you liked for a girl? Tell me."

"Avira. I want to name her Avira. Avira Irene."

"Any particular reason you want that name?"

Zari shrugged and smiled. "Honestly? I just really like vowels."

Emmett laughed. "Well, I like that name. I like that a lot."

"Yeah? Is it settled, then?"

"It is."

SLITHER

~***~

"It says here to connect slat C1 with bar A2." Zari was reading the instructions for the assembly of the baby crib out loud to Emmett, who was sitting on the floor of their bedroom surrounded by tools, nuts, bolts and a multitude of wooden pieces and feeling frustrated beyond belief.

"There is no slat called C1. I've looked at all of them." Anger flushed his cheeks and seemed to deepen the lines that had settled around his eyes. Anger was getting to be the only emotion he had that he recognized. He hated himself for it, and held tight to it, just the same.

"It has to be there, Emmett. Look again. Here, I'll help." Carefully, Zari lowered her ever expanding body onto the floor, grunting a little as she dropped the last few inches with the grace of a drunken giraffe. Sorting through the mountain of pieces that was somehow supposed to eventually resemble a crib, Zari attempted to locate the missing slat of wood. Emmett was right. It wasn't there. Leaning back onto her elbows, Zari peered under the bed. "I think I see one under here. It must've gotten kicked over this way somehow." Reaching her arm beneath the bed and grabbing the errant piece, she pulled it out and read the tiny print carved into the bottom of it. "Yeah. This is C1. Here you go."

None too gently, Emmett grabbed it out of her hand and threw it across the room, where it smacked the wall and bounced back down on the floor. "Great! How about you just put the whole damn thing together by yourself then? I'm done!" He stormed from the room, his heavy footsteps on the staircase echoing in her ears. Startled, tears sprang to her eyes and she wiped them away with the edge of her sleeve. These angry outbursts of his were becoming all too common, and it seemed to Zari that each passing day the man she'd fallen in love with disappeared a little more, replaced by the harsh personality that had overtaken Emmett. With the baby due in less than a month, she was beginning to worry Emmett may not be able to handle fatherhood. The erratic mood swings had begun to frighten her with their intensity, and he was constantly yelling about something or other. *I can't remember the last time he seemed like himself. How can I fix this? I want my husband back.* Holding the bed frame to help drag her heavy body up, Zari took a few deep breaths to help stop her tears and headed downstairs. Finding Emmett in the kitchen making coffee, she walked up behind him and slipped her arms around his chest, squeezing. "I love you," she said simply, and waited. Emmett sat his cup of coffee on the counter and dropped his head, bringing his hands up to cover Zari's. "I love you, too," he said with a tired sigh. He was tired of constantly battling himself and hated the person he knew he was becoming but felt powerless to stop it. Turning to Zari, he drew her to him with one hand behind her back and one behind her head. Settling his chin on her shoulder, he whispered, "I'm sorry. I don't know what is wrong with me."

"Emmett, I—" Pain struck her, a hot, clutching spasm of agony wrapping around both sides from her spine to the center of her abdomen. Worse than the force of Nan's boot in her stomach and she closed her eyes against both the current pain and the miserable memory it brought. "Oh!" she cried out, bending over. Her face twisted and reddened.

"What is it? What's wrong?" Guilt and fear washed over him, thick and oily.

"It hurts." The two words sputtered out between gasps.

"I don't know what to do. What do I do?" Even as he said it, Emmett was pulling a dining table chair over for Zari to sit in, and he helped guide her into it. "Should I call the doctor?"

Zari dug her fingers into Emmett's shirt, twisting it. Emmett knelt before her, his eyes soft and face tender, real. "Tell me how to help, babe." *Babe. It's been so long since he called me that.* The pain began to dissipate, ebbing slowly into easier to handle waves. Zari blew out the breath she'd been holding, spent.

"I'm not sure, but I think that was a contraction." She flinched at a twinge of residual pain.

"A contraction? It's too early!" His voice wavered, frightened and repentant.

"As long as I don't feel any more of them, I think it was one of those Braxton-Hicks contractions. The doctor warned me this might happen. It just means my body is getting ready for the birth. It's okay." Zari licked her lips and blew out a deep breath.

"You're sure?" The pitch of his voice had risen several decibels.

"I'm not sure of anything. This is my first time through a pregnancy. But that felt how the doctor described it to me." She felt raw and irritated; angry about his outburst upstairs and simultaneously wishing he would hold her close, now, and somehow take the pain away.

"I hate to see you in pain." Emmett's tone had lowered; his words now were deep and dusky with emotion.

"The birth will be worse. You'll have to get braced up for it." *You think you're worried about the pain, buddy.*

"I'm worried about more than the birth." Emmett stood and grabbed another chair, bringing it over so he was sitting directly across from Zari.

"So am I." Deciding to take a chance since he seemed so much himself for the moment, she added, "I'm worried about *you*. What's happened, Emmett? You've changed so much. It frightens me."

He laughed, but it was not a cheerful sound. "What's happened? Can you honestly ask me that question, Zari? We're about to have a baby that your family and some snake god I don't understand wants to steal away from us. It makes no sense to me and I can't understand it. I can barely believe it's true and not some elaborate...no. I know you're telling me the truth. It's just, I don't have any idea how to protect us from whatever the hell is coming, and what's coming could happen at any moment. I can't sleep. I feel so panicked all the time. Look, Zari. My mother was an addict. My whole life I've been worried I carry that gene, that weakness. What if her problems started like this? I feel like I'm losing my mind. I want to be a better parent than she was. I want to give our daughter everything, but I don't even know if I can protect her when she's born. And even if I can figure out a way to keep her safe, what if I end up like my mother? What if I totally fail?" His voice cracked and he cleared his throat and coughed in an attempt to cover it. Emmett stood and straightened his shoulders, rubbing his face with his hand. "The pressure is killing me."

"You will never be like your mother, Emmett. You have always been a good husband, and you'll be a good father. I know it. Your mother didn't even try to protect you from that monster, and you're already worried about keeping our baby safe. Our child isn't even here yet, and you're a thousand times better parent to her than your mother ever was for you. I trust you. I believe in you. I know you can do this. *We* can do this. We have to find a way to keep her safe."

"I'm sorry I've been such a prick." Might as well admit it. He'd seen her face when he'd thrown the piece of wood, and she looked afraid. Afraid of *him*. After all he'd promised her, failing, it seemed, was what he did best. His shoulders slumped forward and his jaw clenched. And there his fingers went – *tap-tap, tap, tap, tap.*

"You *have* been a pretty big prick. I miss *you*. This guy you've been lately, so cold and angry. I want *my* Emmett back." Her voice trembled. Zari worked to keep her mouth straight, though her chin wobbled.

"I'll try harder. I will." Emmett leaned in to kiss her, brushing his hand against her hair. A knock sounded on the front door. "Who in the world?" Emmett stood to answer it, and Zari followed, albeit at a much slower pace. He looked through the window and glanced back at Zari. "It's Jessa. Did you know she was coming over today?"

"Oh. Yeah, she said she had something for the baby and might stop over with it this week."

Emmett winced. Jessa was a nice enough girl, but since the day she'd seen his bare back, he'd felt incredibly uncomfortable around her. Working hard at his recent promise to Zari, he smiled at Jessa who was standing on the front porch with flakes of snow peppering her long dark hair and holding a pink gift bag in her hand. Jessa held his gaze a beat too long to be considered comfortable. "Hey Jessa. Come on in out of that cold." Emmett stepped aside to allow her in. Zari closed the gap between them and gave her friend a hug.

"Hey girl! I've missed you!"

"Missed you too. Look, I've brought you something." Both women sat down on the couch, Zari holding one arm around her belly.

"I love presents. Give it to me," Zari giggled.

Handing her offering over, Jessa said, "I'm sorry it took me so long to finish. I've been working on this and about a million other projects. You know how that goes."

"Do I ever. All right, I can't wait any longer. Let's see what we've got here." Gently pulling out the pink and purple tissue paper, Zari peeked at the bottom of the bag. "Oh, Jessa," she breathed as she pulled the crocheted blanket out, dropping the bag on the floor. "This is amazing. Emmett, look what Jessa made for Avira." Lavender and turquoise yarn was combined in a complicated, circular pattern. It was warm and sturdy, but had a delicate, lacy feel that was decidedly feminine. The blanket had a radius of approximately sixty inches and was absolutely breathtaking. "I've never seen a circle blanket like this before! I love it! Thank you."

"That's pretty, Jessa," he said politely. "How thoughtful of you. Would you ladies like some tea?" At their nods, he headed into the kitchen to fix two cups of liquid warmth, picking up his now lukewarm coffee and sipping it as he went.

"Hey. I've got to go to the bathroom, *again*. I'll be back in a minute." Laboriously, Zari struggled to her feet, bracing her hands against her lower back to keep herself upright.

"No worries. I'll hang around a little longer." Zari waddled down the hallway to the bathroom, and Jessa felt uncomfortably alone in the big living room. She wandered into the kitchen to see if Emmett needed help with the tea, and almost convinced herself that was the real reason. But as she stood in the doorway, she quietly admired him while he moved about in the kitchen. Emmett felt her standing there and waited a beat to see if she left. She didn't. Frustrated and instantly angry, he spun and walked toward her briskly, slamming his hand into the wall above her shoulder. Nearly nose to nose, Jessa was instantly intimidated and shrank back against the wall. Emmett looked so different. Irritation crossed his face and his usually bright blue eyes were hard and cold. He spoke through his teeth, jaw twitching as he did so. "I don't know what your problem is, Jess, but I would appreciate it if you would *stop staring at me*. Every time you're here, you're gawking at me and I'm sick of it. I'm not a freak, and you need to just get over the scars you saw on my back. Just *forget it.* You understand me?"

Ashamed but thankful he hadn't figured out the true reason for her fascination for him, she nodded. "I'm sorry," she whispered.

"Guys? Where are you at?" Zari had walked back into the living room and found it empty. Red-faced, Jessa stumbled from the kitchen and smiled weakly at Zari. "Hey, I just remembered I've got to do something. I, um, I've got to go, hon. I'm glad you like the blanket." Grabbing her coat up in her arm, Jessa slammed the door as she left. Zari blinked at her husband. "What was that about?" He shrugged. "Who knows? Are you ready to get that crib finished? Come on." Up the stairs they went, on much better terms than when they'd come down them.

From its hiding place in the crack between the bottom of the hall closet door and the floor, the snake watched, its forked tongue slipping in and out of its mouth.

~***~

Zari was dreaming about the baby. Her round, warmly fuzzy head was nestled in the crook of Zari's arm, damp with sweat, and the child was nursing. The hungry, insistent mouth sucked eagerly. The small, warm tongue helping the milk to flow and fill the round cheeks before the infant swallowed the nourishing liquid. There was an easy rhythm to the action: tongue, suck, fill, swallow. Zari's breast was hot and swollen, hard and heavy with milk that had waited too long to be expressed and the child's willingness to nurse brought a sort of painful relief that caused Zari's eyes to smart with wetness. The baby's eyes fluttered as she fought sleep. Milk drunk, Zari thought, and smiled tenderly at her daughter. Realization that she was feeling teeth gently biting into her nipple startled her and she pulled back, separating herself from the child. Milk dribbled from the red little mouth, and as the baby yawned and started to shove her fist into her mouth, Zari noted the toothless pink gums. A tiny, forked tongue poked from the infant's lips and a high, hissing sound filled Zari's ears. Gasping, she opened her eyes. Curly, dark brown hair spilled over her swollen breast, the blue lines of veins immediately beneath the skin visible in the dim light of morning. Instantly, her hand slipped behind Emmett's head, drawing him closer, wishing he could take it deeper into his mouth. "Emmett," she whispered urgently, pressing toward him so that her breast puddled, fat and fleshy, against his face. He opened his mouth wider, taking more of her into the warm wetness within. His tongue swirled around her nipple and she groaned. Zari roused herself awake, thinking he wanted more and ready if he did. But he was content there, curled against her, sucking. His hand rested lightly on her hip. There was something intrinsically precious and fulfilling for her in what he was doing and she pressed harder against him, murmuring words of love and encouragement to her husband. The feel of her breast in his hot mouth, with her grossly swollen belly between the two of them, his body curved around the mound of their daughter, was so brilliantly sweet it caused an ache deep in her core. Inside her, the child tumbled and kicked lazily. Zari felt for a moment that all three of them were connected and wished she could suspend time for just a little longer, holding on to that intense, almost groggy feeling of safety and love, stretching it out like a quilt of protection around her family.

    She brushed her mouth against Emmett's forehead, kissing him, using her hand to move some of his dark hair up off of his forehead, so she could see his face. He looked so peaceful there, his eyes closed so that his lashes swept downward, then curled up. She could see the hard outline of his cheekbone, and his jaw working gently as he suckled. "Don't stop," she whispered. "It's the only way I can be inside you, and I want to fall asleep this way."

Valarie Savage-Kinney

Chapter Eleven

Hissing Echoes.

"There is a stubbornness about me that never can bear to be frightened at the will of others. My courage always rises at every attempt to intimidate me."

— Jane Austen, *Pride and Prejudice*

The pain was unbelievable: searing, blinding knives through her mid-section. Her hips felt as if they were shattering within her. *Wake up wake up wake up.* The nightmare had been horrific, the pain in her abdomen not as terrifying as the dream of snakes covering her head, her face, dipping in and out of her nose, ears, and mouth. The hissing sound surrounded her, wet and so incredibly loud it echoed through her bones. As Zari's eyes snapped open, sickness welled in her stomach alongside the pains. She struggled to find her voice as she fought to fully wake. There was a tightness across her neck that restricted her breath, and panic rose in her throat. Zari was awake now, fully awake and the realization of what was happening pierced her heart with icy fear. She was in labor. They were not alone in their bedroom, and somehow – through some horrendous magic that could only be attributed to Slither – her dreads were alive, hissing. Several were moving on their own in the air above her head, and others had wrapped around her throat, constricting more and more with each struggle for breath. "Em…Emmett," she whispered, clutching the dreads cutting off her air supply with one hand and slapping at her sleeping husband with the other. "What? What's going on?" He sat up fast, rubbing the sleep from his eyes as he tried to acclimate his vision to see in the darkness. His heart began to thud erratically in his chest as he noted the shadows in the bedroom were not the residue of a dream. Three figures surrounded their bed and he shot his gaze to Zari, who was arching her back in abject agony, the contractions coming ever closer as she struggled for air. Unable to believe what he was seeing: actual snakes coming out of her head, tightening around her throat, Emmett paused for a moment as he took in the situation. This was really happening. They were here. And they were trying to kill Zari.

They were here to take their baby.

"NO!" The word ripped from his throat, roaring in passion and hatred. Bracing one hand against Zari's shoulder, he took the other and grabbed the snakes that were strangling her, pulling with all his might. Finally, the serpents snapped in half and he could hear their high-pitched, dying hisses as they crumbled to ash in his hand. Zari gasped for air. "Emmett. The baby is coming." Having to guess, the contractions were maybe two to three minutes apart, gruesomely aggressive, and rapidly gaining speed, coming closer together faster than she could have imagined. Back labor made her feel as if she was ripping apart in several directions. Spasms of pain clenched about her spine in cruel twists that left Zari wondering how women throughout history had possibly survived such brutality. But that was the least of her problems at the moment.

One shadow had come around Zari's side of the bed, yanking Zari's T-shirt up and placing cold hands against her bare skin. "Get back!" Emmett shouted. "Don't touch my wife!"

The shadow stood fast, then spoke in the darkness to the other shadow people. "Contractions are strong, but being her first, we might have to wait awhile for the child to arrive. Of course, I could save us all the trouble and just cut it out." The gravelly voice spoke as if she were discussing a trip to the supermarket.

"I said get back! Take your hands off of her!" Emmett was livid, shaking with rage, his voice like a living thing filling the room with intensity.

"Or what, Emmett? What will you do to us? Nothing." Nan was nonplussed. She waved her hand toward him as if he was nothing more significant than a gnat.

The lights flicked on, and Emmett saw a figure near the door. A smaller, younger version of Zari leaned against the door frame. He took in the scene: the older woman with her hands all over Zari's belly. That had to be her Nan. The man standing nearest to Emmett's place on the bed was her father. And the mousy woman in the ragged brown sweater and the stringy brown hair was her mother. Now that he knew who the threat was, he took action. "What I'm going to do is kill every last one of you. And enjoy the pleasure of it." He spoke each word carefully, deliberately slow to be sure they understood his intent.

Pop spoke. "You think you can kill us? How? There are more of us, and we bring the power of Slither. You cannot win this, Emmett." Incredulous, Pop smiled wryly at the nerve of his son-in-law.

Zari cried out, another contraction assaulting her body. The women were unconcerned with the exchange between the men. Nan turned to her daughter, "Check her. If she's close enough, we'll let her deliver naturally and save ourselves the mess. We'll kill her once the child is born."

"Mama! No! Please don't take my baby!" Zari's voice was

pitiful. This was the greatest threat of her life and she was absolutely helpless to do anything. Even as she cried out, the pressure between her thighs was so heavy she felt she could not possibly bear any more pain. Her spine was twisting in misery. She was screaming through her teeth now, a high, eerie keening noise that reverberated up Emmett's spine, leaving him chilled with sweat.

Emmett jumped from the bed to the floor. He was taller than Zari's father and looked down on him, cold menace lining his features. As he formulated a plan in his mind, Pop knocked him across the face with a right hook, sending Emmett stumbling back into the bed. Immediately, he felt his mouth fill with a quick gush of hot blood, and reached a hand up to his lip, checking the damage. Instantly, the split lip began to swell and the fingers touching his mouth became damp and sticky. Emmett blinked. So much was happening in just the space of what seemed a few seconds and Emmett was still struggling to get his bearings. He stared at the man, watching as his face morphed from that of Zari's father to Aaron's features, and back again.

"No, Aaron," he said, his words biting the air. "I. Said. *NO!*" Startled, Pop's eyes squinted in confusion. "Who...?" Pop began, but was immediately cut off. Emmett was aware of a hideous roaring sound. He wondered for a ridiculous moment if these people could shift into bears as well. His mind was clear now, though, and he was back on his feet immediately, kicking Pop behind the knees and placing his hands around Zari's father's throat as the man toppled to the floor. Pop's face reddened and his eyes widened as Emmett's hold tightened. "I said no! No, you cannot have me again! No, you cannot have my wife or my child!" Emmett's eyes worked to focus on the man, furious as he continued to flash back to his childhood. "No, no, NO!" He could feel, clearly *feel*, Aaron's soft hands on his body, lightly stroking his bare flesh, feel the weight of his abuser on his back. With undeniable clarity, he felt Aaron's body shifting as he loosened his muscles, readying to take the whip to Emmett's skin. He could smell the scent of Aaron's cigarettes pervading the air of the bedroom and unintentionally arched his back away from the burn he sensed coming. Yet consciously, he *knew* this was Zari's father, and he knew the reason he was there. No longer was Emmett weak or afraid. "You come into my home. You threaten my family and expect me to sit back and take it? You are sadly mistaken, *Dad*." Pop smacked at Emmett's arms, his air supply quickly dwindling as the younger, larger man sat atop him with one knee pressing down with all his weight on Pop's chest. He had vastly underestimated the power of Emmett's youth, strength, and sheer willpower to protect his family. "I am not a child any longer!" Emmett drew back a powerful, muscular arm and relished the feel of his fist smashing into the center of Pop's face. Beneath his knuckles, he felt a distinct *crack*, and smiled at the sudden curvature in what was once a straight nose. Back he drew his arm again, and straight into Pop's face plowed his fist. And again. Once more. Blood gushed from Pop's mouth and nose; a black, sticky fluid that clung to Emmett's hand. The horrifying roaring sounded once again in his ears and as Pop went limp on the floor, Emmett leaped to a half-crouched position, animal-like, scanning the room. He realized his throat burned, and his mouth was open. The threatening growls were coming from his own body.

Mama had crawled up onto the bed between Zari's legs, unceremoniously yanking her underwear off and peering at Zari with detached interest. Cold fingers manipulated Zari's painfully swollen perineum, and she kicked at her mother with as much strength as she could muster. "Stop it! No!" Zari's face was damp, shimmering with tears and sweat.

Nan spoke. "Gianna. Come hold your sister's legs still." Gianna grinned, flicking her forked tongue out and licking her lips, and then climbed onto the bed, clenching Zari's legs with her hands. She hated Zari so much. Her older sister had caused them nothing but trouble ever since she could remember. Learning Nan planned to kill her once the kid was out was pure joy, as far as Gianna was concerned. Listening to Zari scream in pain filled Gianna with unencumbered happiness. Mama looked up from her task and nodded at Nan. "She's crowning. It's time for her to push."

Zari tried to fight it. The desire to push overwhelmed her, but she fought the urge for as long as possible. Her body was determined to evict her baby, but Zari knew to deliver now meant death for her, for Emmett, possibly even for the baby. Her efforts bought a few moments, but not long. As she screamed in pain and fear, dreads-turned-snakes still circled her head and a hot gush of liquid burst forth from her body, drenching the quilts. "Ew! Gross!" shouted Gianna, scrunching her face up in disgust. Without her consent, Zari's body began bearing down, the pressure unbelievable and the process unavoidable. However, the brief delay had occupied the women of her family long enough that they didn't realize Emmett had won the battle with Pop, whose limp body lay on the floor near the bed. He wasn't dead and Emmett knew it, but he was certainly out of commission for a few minutes and that gave Emmett a moment to think. As he rose from their skirmish on the floor at the side of the bed, he took note of the three women mishandling his writhing wife: Nan in the center, between Zari's legs, a garish smile on her face as she waited for the arrival of his daughter. Gianna and Mama each held one of Zari's legs up and back, and Zari strained with the pressure of pushing through the pain, gulping air between pushes. Sweat and tears mixed together and dripped from her pale face, and the damn snakes that used to be her hair swirled around her head like Medusa. Unreal. But he couldn't stop, and he knew his course of action as soon as his eyes landed on it. Zari cried out, a horrifying, strangled sound that sounded like she was dying, and the three women surrounding her all bent in to get a closer look at the baby's head that was slowly arriving, face up.

    Taking advantage of their inattentiveness, Emmett leaped onto the bed and up, grabbing his grandfather's sword from its place on the wall and kicking up, shoving his foot from the wall for power and leverage as he yanked the blade from its scabbard. Waving it out, Emmett brought the sword down and through with all the power he had within him, slicing through Nan's neck. He shivered as her head rolled off and onto the floor, spraying black blood all over Zari and the other two women. Before they could comprehend what had happened, his sword had chopped off Mama's head without even a glimmer of hesitation. Gianna screamed and tried to crawl from the bed, but Emmett, grunting and growling like a rabid dog, was on her in an instant, grabbing ahold of her hair and yanking her head back, baring her throat to him before the blade set to its gruesome job and when it had, Emmett stood for a second, disgusted by the head he held in his hand and his own actions. Acid rose unbidden to his throat and he grimaced, swallowing and forcing it back down. He dropped the head on the mattress and shoved the decapitated bodies off and onto the floor.

    Pop was beginning to stir; he moaned briefly, then began to mutter in a low voice, "Serpentine god, we ask your protection." Emmett knelt down next to him, and whispered, "Threatening my family was your first mistake. Not believing I would kill you was your second. " As Pop's eyes opened, he watched with stunning clarity as the silver twinkle of the sword came at him, then felt it continue through the flesh of his neck. White light shot from his eyes as death consumed him. Breathing hard, Emmett stood, victorious, bloody and pumped on adrenaline. "Emmett! Help me!" Zari's voice broke through the murderous haze and he dropped the sword, kicking past the bodies on the floor to get to her side. She was up on her elbows, gasping as she prepared to push for the final time. Zari shook with the odd sensation that gripped her. She felt abruptly that she'd been plucked from time itself and hung in a strange limbo. There was no time before her, and none ahead. There was only right now, this instant, and her skin felt as raw as if her nerve endings had risen past her skin and quivered, awaiting a flogging. Her bare legs were peppered with splatters of blood and the bed was soaked with amniotic fluid, the blood of her family members, and shit. "What do I do?" His chest pounded from exertion, and he fought to calm himself. He wanted to kill more. Emmett breathed hard, his chest caving in with the force of each breath. He clenched and unclenched his fists. He looked to his wife for guidance.

"Just help her out…when I push." The horror she'd just witnessed was traumatizing, but her only goal was helping her daughter into the world safely. Despite the horror surrounding her, Zari – like millions of women before her, regardless of time or status – was singularly focused on delivering her baby. In that moment, she felt one with those nameless women of history: peasant and princess, crofter and queen. They were all the same in that moment of blood and sweat and tears, unified through time and struggle. "I'm ready." Tucking her chin to her chest and taking a deep breath, she held it in as she grabbed her thighs, pulling them toward her chest as she pushed – down, down, down -- for all she was worth. When it seemed she had no more strength, no more breath, no more possible ability to try at all, Zari felt the blessed relief of the terrible pressure once the baby left her body, and despite the violent wreckage surrounding them, she was filled with euphoria. Stunned, Emmett's hands tugged just a little bit as he guided his daughter into the world. "She's here, Zari. She's here!" Smeared in mucus and blood, the little girl laid frighteningly still in Emmett's large hands. Worried, Emmett met Zari's eyes. "She's not moving or...or crying or anything."

Zari closed her eyes, thinking hard about the books she'd read in preparation for the birth. "Wipe her mouth out. Use your finger and clear all the mucus from her mouth." Shaking, Emmett tucked the baby into his chest like a football and used his opposite hand to clear the thick, sticky fluids from in and around her tiny mouth. She was so terribly small, so fragile and delicate in his large hands. Emmett experienced a jolt of fear that he had inadvertently injured the child with his strength. Cautiously, he jiggled her a bit in his arms. "Come on, baby. Come on. Wake up." A sob escaped Zari as she waited in the silence.

Abruptly, the child began to wail and wave her arms. Emmett grinned at his wife. "We've got to clean you two up and get you to the hospital." Zari reached her hands toward him, and he set the precious bundle down on her chest. In that second only the three of them existed in the world. Zari began to weep as she placed her hands on her daughter: one on the little girl's back and one behind her small round head. She whispered two words over and over. "Thank you, thank you, thank you, thank you, thank you." A sudden panic seized Zari and she gently used her finger to open the baby's mouth—she sighed with relief when she saw her daughter's tongue was *not* forked. The momentary cloud of joy Emmett had been wrapped up in began to dissipate as a whining, hissing sound permeated the room and his eyes darted to the headless bodies on the floor, simultaneously snatching the sword back up in his hand.

In horror Emmett realized the source of the hissing. From the raw, jagged and bloodied stumps that once held the heads of the deceased, rose fat, slimy black snakes. "Sweet Mother of –" startled, his voice rose several decibels. "Mother fu—" he began again. Overwhelmed and exhausted, Emmett seemed unable to latch onto and finish any expletives he started. "What the—? Sweet Jesus! *Shit, shit!*" The tiny, scaly heads pushed slowly through the tangled mess of muscles, tendons, and arteries and as they moved, the skin of the fallen toughened, turning before Emmett's eyes from pasty human flesh to scaled snake skin. Emmett roared as he took on the new threat, dashing first to Nan's body and driving the sword to sever the writhing serpent head, then jamming the blade down the inside of the snake and yanking up, splaying both the narrow body of the serpent and the flesh of Nan's neck and chest wide open. He recoiled only briefly at the fresh spew of viscous black blood before moving on to do the same with the other three bodies. As the last snake was sliced open, the hissing dreads on Zari's head quieted, magically returning to her normal hair. Once stilled, his mind began to race at the thought of disposing of the massacre. What he desperately wanted to do was just take Zari and the baby to the hospital and leave the mess for later. Concerns about Zari's heart condition and bleeding disorder nattered at his brain until he could barely think straight, but he worried about someone accidentally coming upon the gruesome scene while they were gone. His mind searched for solutions even as he stepped over the crumpled heaps that were once Zari's family, picking a dark blue button-down shirt up off the floor and brought it to Zari, tucking the fabric around the baby. He ran a filthy hand through his hair, then winced at the action. A thought popped into his head – the snakes during the storm. Grady had said they'd poured something – had it been bleach? - on them and the bodies had burned themselves up. It was worth a shot, and without a word he turned and ran down the stairs, across the living room and down into the basement, careening into the utility room and grabbing two bottles of bleach off the table. Back up the stairs he went, out of breath as he returned to the bedroom. Uncapping the bottles as he walked, he held the bleach high and poured it over Nan's body. Flinching at the immediate stench as her snakelike flesh began to disintegrate and turn to charred ash, Emmett continued his mission. His stomach boiled as he drizzled bleach on the disembodied heads and watched as they, too, crumbled into hard, blackened bits. Zari pulled herself to a slightly more upright position and watched as he did his disgusting work. "Is it…are they…going away?"

"Yes. Let me finish cleaning this up quick, and we've got to get you to the hospital. Is she doing okay?" His voice was flat. So many emotions threatened to overwhelm him, he fought to hang on to his hardened exterior. He pressed his lips together firmly.

"She seems to be. I want the doctor to check her out, though."

"I'm going as fast as I can. I'm going to run downstairs for the shovel and a couple trash bags. Will you be all right?"

"Yeah."

Again, Emmett left the room running. Moments later, he returned with the tools he needed to finish his task. The baby screamed while he worked, and Zari bounced her against her chest, cooing to the infant. Emmett shoveled the chunks of what now resembled burned wood into the trash bags, tying them tight once they were full and leaving once more with a bag in each hand to dispose of them in the outside cans. Stopping only to wash his hands quickly in the bathroom sink, he grabbed his keys from the table and clicked the key fob to start Zari's car and get it warmed up. One task at a time. If he looked ahead at all, he couldn't think straight. Back in the bedroom, Emmett opened the bottom drawer of the armoire and pulled out two more quilts. "It's cold out. I've got the car started, but we'll just wrap you guys up in these. Um…Zari? I didn't think, but should we…I mean, should I cut the cord?"

"I haven't pushed the placenta out yet. I think we're supposed to leave it intact."

"Okay, then. Can you stand?"

"I think so." Wobbly, Zari sat up and swung her legs over the side of the bed, still holding her daughter tight to her chest. The child's cries had settled down to just whimpers, and Zari swaddled the little girl more securely in the blue dress shirt and pulled the quilts from Emmett's hand to wrap around herself. "Let's go." As Zari attempted to stand, the blood drained from her face and she began to tilt. Emmett's arms were around her in an instant. "I'll just carry you both." With one strong arm around Zari's back and the other beneath her knees, Emmett scooped his family up and tentatively started down the stairs. Taking each step with caution, he made certain his feet were steady before taking another. Finally, they'd made it to the living room and Emmett continued his trek to the front door, leaning his bundle against the wall for an instant so he could open the door and get his keys out of his pocket. Resuming his stance, he carried his wife and daughter outside, through the dusting of snow that was quietly falling and into the waiting car.

As they backed out of the drive, Zari turned to her husband and said, "Thank you, Emmett. I was so afraid, but you were amazing. I still can't believe everything that just happened."

Dropping one hand from the steering wheel, Emmett cleared his throat and spoke. "I told you what would happen if they came for you, and I meant it. I will protect you with my life. And I am so proud of you, Zari. Look at what you did tonight! In the middle of that nightmare, you brought our daughter into the world. She's so beautiful, just like you."

"She is beautiful, isn't she?" Tenderly, she smiled down at her daughter.

"Yes. Zari, do you think it's over? Now that your family is dead, will Slither come back for you again?" He attempted, and failed, to keep the worry from his voice.

"I don't know. I hope not. If it does, we'll fight again." Steel determination could be heard in her words.

"Damn straight we will fight. But sweetheart, if something happens and your dreads turn into snakes again…"

"Yeah?"

"Can we just shave them off? Because that was beyond horrifying." Grimacing, Emmett shivered.

For the first time since the ordeal had begun, Zari burst into laughter.

Chapter Twelve

Perfect Imperfection.

*"I feel all right
Like the morning,
I am golden
Can't stop the wonders
From happenin' around me."*
-Mike Himebaugh, *Golden*

Emmett walked back into Zari's hospital room, rubbing his hands together. "Nurse says as soon as the doctor signs off, we can leave. He should be down any minute."

"Good. I'll be so glad to go back home. I can't believe she's here, Emmett. Just look at her. She's perfect!" Zari was glowing, adoration for her daughter evident on her face.

"Yes, she is. Just like her mama." Emmett bent down to the car seat and kissed his daughter's head. "I love you, Avira." He kissed Zari. "And I love you, Zari. More than I can even say."

"I love you, too, babe. Look, here comes the nurse."

The brunette in green scrubs handed a pen and paper to Emmett. "You, sign here. She signs down here. Follow up with the doc in six weeks. You guys are free to leave. Let me get your wife into a wheelchair and you are out of here."

"Babe, I'm going to go out and pull the car around. I'll see you in a few minutes."

Zari nodded, fussing with the straps on the car seat and tucking a small quilt around Avira. She leaned in so her forehead touched her daughter's. "Avira Irene, you are so loved. You've got the best daddy in the world."

Just outside the door, Emmett heard his wife's voice and grinned. He had every intention of moving mountains to ensure his little girl grew up safe and happy. Joy swelled in his chest as he walked out the hospital doors to the car. When he drove up to the front of the building, his wife and daughter were waiting with the nurse. He stopped the car and ran around the opposite side to open the back door, and lifted the car seat from Zari's lap to set inside. The nurse stepped forward.

"Are you certain you know how to buckle the seat properly?"

"Yes. I'm sure."

"I'll just wait a moment and double check it before you leave."

Emmett rolled his eyes as he strapped the car seat and its precious occupant into its proper place and stepped back to let the nurse check it out. "All right. Looks good. Best of luck to you, Mr. and Mrs. Delaney." And she was gone.

Zari climbed gingerly into the car, pulling her own seat belt across her chest.

"Ready?"

"Oh, I'm ready. I'm taking my family home."

~***~

SLITHER

"She's crying again." Zari took a long drink of tea and pulled her massive hair back with a band. "I think she's hungry."

"I'll get her. You stay put, babe. Finish your lunch." Scooting back from the dining table, Emmett stood and made his way to the bassinet in the corner of the living room. His voice and eyes softened as he picked up the baby and cradled her in his arms. "Don't cry, baby girl. Sssshhhh." She settled as Emmett bounced her while he walked back to the dining table. "Zari, look how much she's already grown. I can't believe Avira is already a month old."

"I know! But I love seeing her get bigger. Those cheeks!" Zari laughed as she reached out and softly pinched one of Avira's rosy red, plump cheeks. "Her eyes are so pretty. They're the same blue as yours, Emmett."

Emmett grinned. "I know it. She's great. We should do this again!"

"Yeaaaahhhh. Maybe in a couple of years. Let's just try to enjoy Avira for the moment."

Outside, the wind howled and Emmett carried the baby over to look out the front window. "The snow is really coming down out there. I heard we're supposed to get at least another two feet today." Great, fat flakes of snow drifted from the sky, effortlessly settling on the sparkling white earth.

"I'm glad we have no need to go anywhere today. I just want to stay here in our warm, solid home and spend time with you guys. Later on I'm going to pull out that quilt I was working on, finish the binding."

"Sounds good to me. I think we deserve some relaxing, quiet

days after the last few months." Emmett squinted through the window. "What is that? There's something out by your car in the snow. Here, take her. I'm going to go see what it is." He passed off the now-sleeping infant to Zari.

Slipping on his boots, he pulled a sweater from the pegs near the door and shrugged it on. "Back in a sec," he said, and walked out the door into the snow.

Cold, Emmett shoved his hands into his pockets as he walked nearer the object that had been further covered by snow in just the last few minutes. Removing his hands from the warmth of the pockets of his jeans, Emmett crouched down and began unburying the curiosity. Surprised, he clutched it in his hand and carried it back to the house. A rush of frigid air blew into the house as he opened the door back up.

"Babe! Zari, you'll never believe what I found outside!" He stomped the snow from his boots and held his prize in the air. Zari – Avira in arms – came out to the living room at his call.

"What is..." she stopped.

"It's your wreath! Remember, we lost it the first night of those bad storms back in the summer? Look, it's pretty beat up, and half the flowers are gone, but these are your ribbons woven through it, I remember watching when you made it. Somehow, it came back home."

Zari took the wreath gently in her hand, and quite unexpectedly, her face twisted and she began to weep.

"I thought you'd be happy. I didn't mean to make you cry." Watching her face pinch, he felt he'd done something terribly wrong, but couldn't quite figure out what it was. Emmett patted her shoulder feeling useless.

"I am happy. I am." Zari opened the front door and hung her battered wreath back on its nail, unconsciously squeezing the baby closer to her chest as she moved.

"Don't you want to fix it?" Confused, he reached toward the busted decoration.

Zari held her hand up to stop him. "No. It's perfect the way it is." Flawed, beaten and yet…strong, and more beautiful for its imperfection.

It's perfect the way it is.

And she closed the door.

Valarie Kinney is a writer, fiber artist and Renaissance Festival junkie with a wicked caffeine addiction. She resides in Michigan with her husband, four children, and two insane little dogs. She is the author of Slither and Just Hold On.

Visit her blog here:

https://organizingchaosandothermisadventures.wordpress.com/

Visit her Author page here:

http://www.amazon.com/Valarie-Savage-Kinney

Visit the publisher to find more great authors here:

http://twistedcorepress.com/

Made in the USA
Charleston, SC
25 August 2015